SHOOTOUT AT CLEARWATER SPRINGS

River Bow Ranch is in big trouble: owing money to the bank, and with only a small, sickly herd. It looks as if Mark Merkel will be forced to hand over his business to his ruthless neighbour, Connor MacPherson, who has been eyeing the River Bow for some time. But Mark's son David refuses to be defeated, and has an audacious plan to save the ranch. Faced with an implacable enemy, and with a murderer in their midst, can the Merkels succeed?

AARON ADAMS

SHOOTOUT AT CLEARWATER SPRINGS

Complete and Unabridged

LINFORD
Leicester

First published in Great Britain in 2014 by
Robert Hale Limited
London

First Linford Edition
published 2015
by arrangement with
Robert Hale Limited
London

A catalogue record for this book is available
from the British Library.

ISBN 978–1–4448–2642–5

Published by
F. A. Thorpe (Publishing)
Anstey, Leicestershire

Set by Words & Graphics Ltd.
Anstey, Leicestershire
Printed and bound in Great Britain by
T. J. International Ltd., Padstow, Cornwall

This book is printed on acid-free paper

1

'Fourteen hours, fifteen minutes from Carlyle to Clearwater Springs, right on time,' declared the driver as he threw down David Merkel's bag from the roof of the stage.

'Glad I'm not going all the way to Phoenix,' muttered David catching his luggage and hauling the strap over his shoulder. He looked around. In some ways his home town had hardly changed at all. There was the saloon, the store, the bank, the livery stable, all much as they were when he left nearly five years ago. The only difference seemed to be they now all bore the name 'MacPherson'. Outside of the main street, though, the town had grown; there were more houses and a church had been built. He trudged towards the saloon.

'Hey, breed, is that you?' he heard a

familiar voice call. He turned swiftly, a smile curling the corners of his lips.

'Paulie MacPherson,' said David. 'You haven't changed at all, more's the pity.'

Paulie laughed, slapped David on the shoulder and pulled him into a tight embrace. 'You've gone pale out East, boy. You need some of our Arizona sunshine.'

'I'll be getting plenty, I'm back to stay.'

Paulie's expression seemed sceptical, but he said nothing, other than to offer to buy his friend a beer. The two walked amiably into the saloon.

'Now that is handsome,' said one of the girls to another when she saw David.

* * *

'After fourteen hours and fifteen minutes I needed that,' said David with feeling, downing the cool liquid. He tapped his empty glass on the bar for a refill.

'So what brings you back?' asked Paulie, sipping his drink altogether more conservatively.

David narrowed his dark eyes. 'I've heard your father is determined to take my pa's ranch either by fair means or foul. Thought I'd better check out what's going on.'

'Davy, it pains me to tell you this, but your pa owes the bank an awful lot of money and he ain't making any repayments. River Bow Ranch is going to be forfeit by the end of the month.'

'And, as your father seems to own the bank now, he gets the ranch.'

'Dad owns *everything*, he might as well have the River Bow.'

David's mouth twisted with the struggle to suppress his anger. He didn't share Paulie's conviction that Connor MacPherson had a God-given right to *everything*. He swallowed more beer. 'We'll see what happens,' he snapped, his self-control strained to the limit.

Paulie snorted. 'We'll see nothing,

except by the end of the month the River Bow will be a MacPherson outfit.'

'My sister doesn't agree; she thinks we can save the ranch.'

Paulie's snort was even more derisive. 'From what I've heard things are so bad your sister's working as a ranch-hand. Even worse, there's talk she's given her all to some drifter name of Flynn — '

Paulie said no more as David's fist collided full on with his nose and blood spurted in a vivid cascade from his nostrils. His own hand flailed out, catching David's cheek.

'I'll get the sheriff!' shouted a customer by the door.

The two men threw punches and attempted to fell each other, with fists and feet, until they ended up in an untidy grapple on the floor of the saloon.

The bartender stepped out from behind the bar and, with a resigned sigh, pulled them apart without too much difficulty. 'You two!' he declared.

'Can you never get together without a fight?'

David pulled himself upright and brushed the sawdust from his smart black suit. 'Not while he talks the way he does, no,' he panted, ejecting a jet of red spittle from his mouth. He jabbed his finger at Paulie. 'One more word about my sister, or any other of my kin, and I'll knock your head right off.'

Paulie was likewise dusting himself down. He made a sort of laughing noise, and muttered something about being right, which David, sensibly, chose not to hear.

A tall, skinny man with wire-rimmed glasses burst into the saloon. 'You all right, Mr MacPherson? You want me to put this man behind bars?'

Paulie laughed properly now, and slapped David's back. 'No! This is David Merkel, we're pals from way back. We're just having a friendly scrap, that's all.'

'You sure?' asked the man. 'I don't want to get into any trouble with your father. If this man's attacked you, he should be locked up.'

'It's all right,' said Paulie. 'Davy, let me introduce you to our sheriff, Layton la Bute.'

David merely widened his eyes.

The tall man pulled himself even higher and took a step towards him. 'David Merkel, eh? That makes you a breed. I don't like fighting in this town. I especially don't like fighting Indians, you understand?'

Paulie stepped between them. 'That's enough, Layton. Mr Merkel is an old friend of the family; you treat him with respect.' He turned round, pinching his nostrils. 'Davy, I think you might have bust my nose.'

★   ★   ★

Once out of the saloon David looked around. There didn't seem to be anyone to meet him, so he set off along the trail that led to the ranch. Before long he saw a wagon on the horizon, and was

6

soon pulling himself on board, along-side the driver. 'Still working for my pa then, Stumpy?' he said.

Stumpy raised an eyebrow, as he swung the wagon around. 'Trouble on the journey?'

David felt his lip, which was already swollen. 'Not till I got here. First person I met was Paulie MacPherson. He told me a few things, about the ranch, about Louisa, that I didn't care to hear. He paid for it.'

Stumpy laughed. 'Good to have you back, Young Boss.'

'How bad are things?'

'Not my place to be the bearer of unhappy news, I'll leave that to your sister.'

David leaned back and pulled the brim of his dark hat lower over his eyes.

'Heard you did well out East,' said the hand.

'Worked in a bank.'

'Good! They got no problems with half-breeds out East then?'

'Didn't tell anyone, well not until I

confided in someone I thought I could trust. Then they got problems with me being a breed.'

Stumpy's sigh was heartfelt. 'Was that untrustworthy someone a woman?'

'Reckon it was, Stumpy. Now, get a move on; even these two old nags can move faster than this.'

★　★　★

Paulie was right about one thing: Louisa Merkel did seem to be working as a ranch-hand. She was riding into the yard when he arrived, sitting astride a strong horse and kitted out in working pants, thick waistcoat and wide-brimmed hat and with a six-shooter belted to her waist. She leapt from her mount and ran to David.

'Davy! Davy!' she cried, sobbing into his shoulder and gripping him tightly, then she stood back and wiped the tears from her dusty cheeks.

'For a minute there, I thought I'd got myself a baby brother,' he said, trying to lighten the situation.

'Come into the house, I'll get you something to eat. What happened to your face?'

'Got into a fight with Paulie MacPherson. How's Pa?'

'Drunk or dead drunk.'

On examining his father's room, David realized it was the latter but made no attempt to wake him. He sat at the kitchen table and gobbled some stew and bread while Louisa told him the sorry tale of the last few years.

Mark Merkel had never recovered from the death of his wife. They knew he truly loved her, for it took some courage to marry when society itself was against the match. At first Louisa thought the drinking would subside once her father came to terms with his grief. That never happened. With no one taking control, the ranch deteriorated rapidly. At least half the herd was lost to rustlers, disease or lack of food. She'd tried to pull things round, but it was hard work for a man, never mind a young girl. She'd decided to buy some new stock and that had been her downfall. She borrowed money from the bank.

'Sick, all of them,' she concluded. 'Within two weeks they were dead. I've been around cattle all my life, and believe me, Davy, I saw nothing wrong with them. But, it means we cannot repay the loan. To be fair to Connor, he gave us more time than was strictly necessary, but what's the point? We can't repay today. We can't repay tomorrow.'

David pushed away his empty plate. 'Something I got to ask you. Who's this man, Flynn?'

'Huh! So that's why you fought Paulie! I bet he couldn't wait to tell you I'm a fallen woman.' She snatched his plate. 'We're broke and nearly homeless and all you're bothered about are my morals!' She stomped across the room and threw the plate into the sink. She turned round, her eyes as dark and bewitching as her

brother's, narrowed just as dangerously as his did, the anger in her features souring her beauty. 'Yes I allowed Flynn to have me, *allowed*, mind. He has taken nothing. I love him and I'm going to marry him, and if the world was fair we would stay put and raise our children. But that's never going to happen because Ma died, Pa's always drunk, you went away and everything went wrong. Don't you dare judge me, David Merkel, because I've been here and you haven't. Sometimes I'm so lonely, and then there was Flynn — '
She put her hands to her face and her whole body shuddered as racking sobs convulsed her. David's anger evaporated and he went to her and held her close.

'You have no idea how hard it's been,' she gasped.

He stroked her hair. 'I should never have left you to cope alone. Why didn't you tell me sooner what was happening?'

'The only thing that keeps Pa going is

the success you've made of your life.'

David shook his head sadly.

Louisa disentangled herself from him and vigorously rubbed her eyes with the tea-towel. 'Stupid to cry, it solves nothing.'

'You've earned your tears. It's been too much for a grown man, never mind a girl just past twenty. I'm surprised you kept things going as long as you have.' He reached for his hat and jacket. 'I'd better see what's what for myself. How many hands we got?'

'Five, well six if you count me.'

'Five! You can't run a place like this with five or six hands.'

'I can't afford to pay one let alone more. Those we've got only stay 'cos they've nowhere else to go.'

'Like Stumpy.'

They walked out into the low sunshine. 'Stumpy, Olly, Tom Sackler — '

'They're all still here?'

'Yeah, Caleb too, and then there's Flynn.'

★　★　★

The hands were clustered together around a table in the bunkhouse, sharing a bottle of some amber-coloured liquor. A pleasant-faced middle-aged man came over to David, holding out his hand. 'Welcome back, Young Boss,' he said. 'We're only sorry you've returned to this.'

David returned his handshake warmly. 'Tom, thanks for staying on, thanks to all of you. I hear you've not been paid, I apologize. I intend to fully look into my father's accounts and if there's any way I can recompense you, I shall.'

'There's no money, Davy,' said Louisa.

David didn't answer her. He had some money of his own, and had decided to use that, but he didn't want the men to know. 'You must all feel free to move on to other ranches if you want to.'

'Who'd want a one-armed cripple

13

like me?' said Stumpy.

'Your pa might have too much liking for the bottle,' said Caleb, 'but while he treats negroes the same as everyone else, I'll stay.'

David looked at Tom. 'You're a good foreman; don't tell me you can't get work anywhere else?'

Tom shifted. 'Mr MacPherson has mentioned something. But I'll stick with River Bow till the end. Your pa took me on when I was desperate, with a fondness for gambling and strong liquor. I'll not desert him now he's down on his luck.'

David sighed. He felt all this loyalty was misplaced.

'You ain't asked me why I'm staying,' said Olly.

'No one else could stand your cooking. Young Boss knows that without asking,' said Stumpy, to much amusement, especially from Olly himself.

David's smile was hollow. 'Right, men, carry on doing the best you can.

It's going to take me a couple of days at least to work out what, if anything, I can do. Bear with me, will you.' As there was only one man there that David didn't recognize, he knew who he must be. 'You, Flynn, outside,' he said harshly. Louisa followed them into the yard. 'Go to the house, Louisa.'

'Mr Merkel, my name's Flynn — ' the young man started but David's hand gripped the collar of his shirt and pushed him hard against the wall of the bunkhouse.

'I don't care what you're called, get your stuff and leave now. I've a mind to give you a beating, but I've got better things to do with my time, so just go.'

'I'll take Louisa with me,' said Flynn.

David pulled him away from the wall to get a better aim on the young man's face as his fist swept out and for the second time that day he landed a good square punch. Flynn staggered back, trying to regain his balance. David bent over him and pulled him upright, drawing his arm back for another assault, when he heard a gun cock.

'Don't you dare lay another finger on him, Davy,' snarled Louisa.

He pushed Flynn into the dust, and turned to face her. 'What you going to do, shoot me?'

'I feel like it.'

'You know full well, after what he's done to you, he deserves a whipping at the least.'

'You got this all wrong, Young Boss,' gasped Flynn, pulling himself upright.

'Don't you 'Young Boss' me. Leave this ranch now — ' David jumped as a bullet smacked into the ground by his feet. 'Stop that, you madwoman!' he shouted.

Louisa holstered her gun. 'You ain't worth the lead,' she said. 'Flynn, get your stuff, I'll get mine. We're better off out of this.'

'You stay here,' ordered David.

She turned to walk back to the house, but stopped as a horse careered into the yard and pulled up in a flurry of dust. It was Paulie MacPherson.

'Davy!' he cried leaping from his mount. 'You'd best come into town. It's your grandpappy. He's really gone and done it this time. He's telling everyone he's found gold at Mint Creek.'

2

Clearwater Springs had a new jailhouse with two cells inside. A couple of tatty-looking cowpokes sat in one, listening intently to the small, wizened man who sat in the other.

'Sheriff la Bute,' said David, 'seems you're partial to locking up a man.'

'That might be because I'm the sheriff,' said la Bute, importantly.

'It *might* be. Now, tell me, Sheriff, since when has finding gold been a crime?'

La Bute sidled closer to him, and dropped his voice. 'It's precautionary. If the old fellow has found gold, then I reckoned Mr MacPherson should know first.'

'Of course,' said David. 'You seem to think he's the law here. I haven't been in the church yet, but it wouldn't surprise me to find that MacPherson's

18

set himself up there as the Lord God Almighty.'

'Dad ain't that bad,' said Paulie, who, together with Louisa and Flynn, had followed David into the jail.

Louisa was reaching through the bars. 'We'll get you out, Grandpa,' she said. 'You've done nothing wrong, have you?'

The sheriff looked at David. 'So Dancing Bird is your grandpa?'

David sighed. 'Unless you're going to charge him with some crime, you'd best release him.'

La Bute looked uncertain. 'I'd hoped to speak to Mr MacPherson first, but he's away on business.'

David looked at Paulie. 'Even your father can't imprison people for no reason.'

Paulie twisted his lips, but he couldn't disagree. 'He's right, Sheriff, you'd best let him go.'

'There is no gold,' said David. 'We had prospectors some years back but nothing was found. I expect Grandpa's

19

got a bit confused.'

'I can hear what you're saying, Davy boy, and I ain't confused. I knew you'd come back from the East with your tail between your legs.'

David raised his voice and spoke firmly. 'You're confused about the gold, Grandpa, that's all.'

'I saw what I saw,' said Dancing Bird, pursing his thin, creased lips in a familiar stubborn gesture.

'Please unlock the door,' said Louisa to the sheriff. 'We'll take him back to the ranch. He'll cause you no more trouble.'

'I'm not staying at no ranch,' said Dancing Bird. 'I'm going to get myself a rope and stuff and then I'm going to get myself some gold, pure gold.'

'Just come back for now, have something to eat and a good night's rest. Let's see how you feel tomorrow.' Louisa spoke soothingly as la Bute undid the lock.

'I'm not sleeping in no bed,' said Dancing Bird, 'but I'll not say no to some vittles, even though you cook slops.'

'I'll get his horse from the back,' said la Bute. 'I never got the exact location of the gold, and I gave him quite a thorough interrogation. You're sure he's making it up?'

'Sheriff,' said David, 'if I thought for one minute there was gold up there, I'd go. Believe me, I need it. But there ain't.'

★　★　★

Dancing Bird moaned all the way back to River Bow; years of practice had made him accomplished at it. Nearly everything was the fault of the white man, who had stolen the land, the buffalos and the women. Worst of all was his daughter, who had not only married a white man, but taken on his customs and religion. Even his half-breed grandchildren were no good, not knowing a word of Apache. He never mentioned the fact that he was no longer welcome by his own tribe as they had long since lost patience with his corrosive whining bitterness.

Louisa listened in silence. David tried once or twice to reason with him, but eventually gave up.

David turned his attention to Flynn. 'You still here, then?'

'Don't start,' said Louisa. 'It's getting dark, I'm tired and when we get back I've got to make something for us all to eat. I'd better try and rouse Pa, too, if he's not already drunk himself back to oblivion.'

'Tomorrow then, Flynn, I'll give you till tomorrow to leave. You're under age, Louisa, and in the absence of Pa, you do what I say. Maybe I'll be able to salvage something from the situation.'

Dancing Bird started cackling. 'So you've found out already? Your pa took my daughter, now some white man's stolen his. I'd say that was fair.'

'Nobody seemed to care that I'm underage when I was left running the ranch on my own. You've just got to

22

accept things the way they are, Davy. To put it bluntly, you can't make me a virgin again.'

'If your pa would sober up long enough to give permission, I'd marry Louisa tomorrow,' said Flynn.

'Don't you talk about my father like that,' snapped David.

'You gotta accept what's the truth, Davy boy,' said Dancing Bird. 'Your sister ain't going to be a virgin again, and your pa ain't going to be sober. That's the way of it. I told my girl not to marry him. No good will come of that, I said, and see how right I was. But no one listens to poor old Dancing Bird. Even when I says 'gold' no one listens. You'll see, though. I'll show you.'

David let out a long groan. 'Why didn't I tell la Bute to throw away the key?'

★   ★   ★

Dancing Bird shuffled into the kitchen of the ranch house, and installed himself in the one comfortable chair there, sipping hot coffee and happily chuntering to himself, while Louisa set about preparing some food. Flynn decided to let discretion triumph for the evening and returned to the bunkhouse. David felt it fell to him to see what he could do by way of his father.

Mark Merkel was awake, but lying on his bed looking sightlessly at the ceiling. His eyes did flick towards David when he heard his voice. 'What in tarnation's going on?' he asked.

David couldn't help a smile twist the corners of his mouth. His father still retained a strong Dutch accent, which chimed oddly with the colloquial American he spoke. He put the lamp he carried on the bedside table. 'We're in a mess, Pa. You especially.'

'You on holiday from the bank?'

'No, I left.'

Now Mark sat up. 'And why did you do that?'

'To come and sort you out. Come

downstairs, I'll get some water heated and you can have a bath.'

'And why in tarnation would I need that?'

'Because you stink.'

'Best have a drink first.'

'You'll have a coffee when you get downstairs.'

'You seem to be forgetting who's in charge here. I'll drink what I want and bathe when I have to.'

'Then you'll lose the ranch, Pa.'

Mark swung his legs over the side of the bed. 'No one lost a ranch 'cause there's a whiff about 'em. Your ma was fussy about that, always washing and all. Made me put in that fancy bathroom. She was so proud of that, not that she lived long enough to . . . '

David reached forward and helped his father to his feet. 'So, take a bath as a tribute to Ma, then. Come downstairs and have a coffee. Grandpa's here.'

Mark attempted to return to his bed, David only just managed to stop him; his father was still a strong man.

'Nothing you have said has pleased me at all yet, son. Last thing I want to do is sit chawing with that old idiot Dancing Bird.'

'Come downstairs, Pa, you might find him more interesting than usual. He says he's found gold.'

★   ★   ★

David went to fill the bath while Mark was relatively compliant. Dancing Bird was regaling him about his find, though was careful not to give away any details of the exact location.

Mark sighed and allowed Louisa to refill his coffee cup, he hadn't asked for whiskey for a while. 'Old man,' he said to his father-in-law, 'Stop your chatter. You go back up to Mint Creek tomorrow and take Davy with you. Davy, any sign of gold there you get what you can.'

'Pa, the bank forecloses at the end of the month. I ain't got time to waste riding out with Grandpa and panning for a few grains of gold. I'm needed here.'

'We've managed without you for five years; we can manage another few days. Off you go with your grandpa. Is that water ready yet?'

David accompanied his father to the bathroom and made sure he got in. Once in the warm water Mark lay back and seemed relatively calm.

'We'll go to town tomorrow, you can get yourself a shave and a haircut,' David said to him.

'*I* might. You'll be off at first light to the creek.'

'I ain't taking that half-breed anywhere,' said Dancing Bird, who was peeping round the door.

'Can't I even have a bath in peace without your whining, old man?' snapped Mark.

David handed his father the soap. 'I know you're simply trying to get rid of me so you can get back to your whiskey and lie in bed all day. That ain't going to happen. We're going through your accounts tomorrow, page by page, number by number.'

Mark chuckled.

*   *   *

They ate a similar stew with bread that David had eaten earlier in the day. Louisa said it was one of the few things she knew how to cook. David ate hungrily and Mark made an effort, though he said he couldn't swallow without a drink and poured himself a whiskey. Dancing Bird pushed his food around moaning constantly in mixed-up English and Apache. David was pleased when, at last, everyone decided it was time to call it a day. Dancing Bird went outside to sleep under the stars; everyone else went to their rooms. David was surprised and grateful to see that Louisa had made up the bed for him. He meant to spend some time thinking about the ranch, but instead instantly fell asleep.

* * *

Dancing Bird and his horse had disappeared by the time anyone arose the next morning so David was spared any further argument with his father. In fact Mark emerged from his room at a decent hour and seemed in a relatively sober state of mind. Using the last of the flour and the eggs Louisa and David managed to rustle together some pancakes and for the first time in quite a while the small Merkel family breakfasted together.

'We need supplies,' said Louisa. 'Only problem is money. I think we should sell some of the furniture. We're never going to need Ma's piano again, are we?'

'That instrument stays right where it is,' said Mark firmly.

'I've got money,' said David.

'How much?' asked Mark.

'A few dollars — enough to give the hands something and buy supplies.'

'That's good,' said Louisa. 'I'll make

a list. If you and Pa are going into town, you can go to the general store.'

'Are we going into town?' said Mark, wiping his mouth and pushing his empty plate away.

'You're going to get that haircut and shave.'

'Ah, maybe.'

'No maybe,' said Louisa. 'I'll tell Caleb to get the wagon ready.'

Mark sighed. 'I'm not sure I can do this, even for you, son.'

'Do what?' asked David.

'Make the effort. Even if we keep River Bow, and I don't think we can, it's going to be a long haul. I'm not sure I've got the will.'

David went over to his father and put his hands on his shoulders. 'We gotta try, Pa. Letting MacPherson take over everything, just because he can, ain't right. Not to mention all the hard work you and Ma put into the ranch. You stowed away on a boat when you were fourteen, remember, and came half way round the world to a country where you didn't even know the language. And managed to make a success of yourself. Now why in tarnation can't you cut back on the liquor and help me fight?'

Mark tapped David's hand. 'You're a good man. Too good for this place. Too good for me.' He sighed again, a deep, tired, bitter sigh. 'And you're right, damn you. Always have been.'

★   ★   ★

David went down to the bunkhouse to see what Olly needed by way of supplies and to remind Flynn that he was leaving. Olly knew exactly what he required. Flynn, however, had ridden out early with Tom to check the herd, so David would have to confront him later.

Mark was already in the wagon waiting for him outside. 'I know you want to fight,' he said, as he flapped the reins and gee'd up the horses, 'but I did a load of thinking last night. I suppose I couldn't sleep due to lack of whiskey.'

31

'And?' said David.

'I know you're set against it, but would it be such a bad thing if I let Connor have the ranch?'

'Well, we'd all be homeless and without a livelihood.'

'Not necessarily. What if I could negotiate some sort of deal that kept us on as staff?'

David's expression was sceptical. 'You know MacPherson better than me. Do you think he'd want you, me and the others as hands?'

'Not sure about Stumpy, and I've heard he's no liking for negroes, so Caleb might have to move on, but it still might be the best way. As for your sister, she and that Flynn fellow have a hankering for each other. I reckon they should move on, get themselves a spread somewhere else. There's plenty of land in California, so I hear.'

David crossed his arms. Everything his father said made a certain sort of sense, and yet he felt himself rebelling against it. 'I've sacked Flynn, by the way,' he said. 'He's too familiar with Louisa altogether.'

Mark snorted. 'Then unsack him. We can't go down to four hands just 'cause you're squeamish about a bit of kissing and cuddling.'

'I hate to tell you but it's gone a lot further than that, Pa.'

'Too late, then,' said Mark.

David stared at his father. 'You don't care?'

'Reckon he's as good as she's likely to get.'

David let out a blast of angry air through his lips.

They travelled in silence for a while. 'Do you plan on going back East, son?' asked Mark.

'I wasn't planning to, but if you're so intent on giving the ranch away I'll have to do something. I don't think I fancy working for Connor MacPherson.'

Mark nodded. 'Neither do I. I gotta ask, did you do something bad at the bank? Is that why you gave up your job?'

'No, I was something bad. A half-breed.'

★ ★ ★

By the time David had completed his transactions at the store Mark had finished at the barber's and looked more than presentable. David was reminded of just how handsome his father had once been.

'Seeing as how you've got a few dollars I think you can stand your old man a drink, can't you?'

'I don't think you should be drinking.'

'I don't think you should be tellin' me that.' Mark went into the saloon, forcing David to follow him.

Paulie MacPherson was propping up the bar.

'Do you live here?' asked David, as his father ordered drinks.

Paulie laughed. 'I've been working all morning, I need to wash the dust from my mouth. Where's the old man, gone to get his gold?'

David smiled. 'Quite likely, I wish him luck.'

'It'll be the only thing that saves your ranch.'

'Careful, Paulie, or I'll smack your face again.'

'Is your pa around, Paulie?' asked Mark.

'He should be back tomorrow. He's doing some business in Carlyle at the moment. Think he's trying to persuade the railroad to build a branch line up to Clearwater Springs.'

'Oh, is he now,' said David, quietly and mostly to himself.

Mark seemed to think that was very amusing. 'Clearwater Springs with its own train station? Now that's some ambition.'

'Come on, Pa,' said David, slapping his father's back. 'We need to go to the bank.'

'Do we?' said Mark, but he drained his glass and followed his son outside.

★ ★ ★

'It's the darndest plan,' said David as he paced up and down the kitchen at the ranch house.

'Why did you buy this fowl?' asked Louisa, holding the unplucked bird suspiciously in front of her. 'I don't know what to do with it.'

'Thought it would be something different.'

'I'll put it in the pantry; I'll fry some steaks tonight.'

'Don't you see what MacPherson's doing?'

'Yes,' she said irritably, 'you've explained it perfectly. If he persuades the railroad to build a branch up from Carlyle, it'll have to cross River Bow land. The railroad company will have to buy it — '

'And it will belong to Connor,' finished Mark, puffing heavily on his pipe.

'And Clearwater Springs, which is already owned by MacPherson, becomes a big cow town. Think of the money he'll make.' David sat down and rubbed his face hard, then looked up at Louisa. 'You borrowed money to buy stock, fair enough,' he said to his sister, 'but the interest rate MacPherson's bank is charging is extraordinary. Lou, you said the steers looked healthy but then died, is there any chance they were poisoned?'

Mark sat upright and put down his pipe. 'What are you suggesting, son?'

'Lou's not stupid, she knows a sick cow when she sees one. We've been thinking of Connor MacPherson as greedy and ambitious, and he is, but what if he's more than that? What if he's lost all decency? I'm not saying he's entirely responsible for the state the ranch is in, clearly he ain't, but maybe he noticed how tough things were getting and decided to take advantage of the situation.'

Louisa's eyes widened. 'Surely not, Davy. He's always been a good neighbour to us. He said once if I hadn't had a squaw for a mother, he wouldn't have minded me for Paulie's wife. *I* would have minded, by the way. He paid to have the church built, you know, and pays Pastor Sims as well.'

Mark picked up his pipe again. 'In my experience attending at church ain't never been proof of good character.'

They stopped talking as they heard the front door open and the click of boots on the wooden floor.

'Hello!' called a voice from the hall. It was Flynn.

David got up and went to the door. 'In here, Flynn and I hope you've come to say goodbye.'

'Hold on, son,' said Mark, turning in his chair. 'Come on, Flynn. I hear you've been sacked.'

Flynn came into the kitchen with his head bowed, twisting his hat in his hands.

'Well you're hired again,' said Mark. 'Pour yourself a drink, lad.'

David breathed deeply and looked at the ceiling. 'Pa,' he started, but Mark silenced him with a wave of his hand.

Flynn didn't avail himself of Mark's

offer, though Louisa did get a glass for him. Flynn coughed slightly. 'Mr Merkel, sir, glad to see you're better, sir.'

'Never knew I was ill,' said Mark. 'Got a little too friendly with the liquor for a while, and doubtless will do again. You look like you've something on your mind; best say what it is.'

'It's just, Mr Merkel, Boss, well it's like this. I'd like to marry Louisa.' He stopped and poured himself the drink now, and knocked half of it back in one go. 'I'd be grateful it we could have your permission.'

Mark smiled. 'Am I supposed to ask you what your prospects are?'

David filled his glass with whiskey now. 'Flynn's prospects are the same as all of ours: bankruptcy and homelessness. Pa, don't agree to this.'

Louisa banged her hands on the table. 'Davy, can't you bear to see me happy?'

'I'd like to see you with a man that respects you, that's all.'

Mark stood up, went over to Flynn and shook his hand. 'If you're prepared to be part of this family, you have my blessing to marry Louisa. Just don't expect me to pay for a big wedding.'

Flynn pumped Mark's hand, offering him profuse and heartfelt thanks. Louisa ran over and hugged both of them. She looked down at her brother, sipping his drink morosely. 'Please be happy for me, Davy,' she pleaded.

'Come on, son, lighten up,' said Mark, chuckling happily. 'All right, Flynn's been a tad more familiar with my daughter than he should have been, but he's doing the decent thing. And remember he'll have Dancing Bird as his grandpappy-in-law. Surely that's punishment enough for any liberties he's taken.'

3

Louisa and Flynn went into town first thing to see the pastor; there seemed no reason to wait to arrange their wedding.

David was surprised to see the scrawny figure of Dancing Bird scuttling around the yard, his long, matted, grey hair swinging limply. David called him over. 'You given up on the gold, Grandpa?'

'Ain't none of your business. I shouldn't have told anyone, especially not you.'

'Louisa's marrying that no-good Flynn, if you're interested.'

Dancing Bird shrugged. 'She'd never make a proper squaw anyway, best she goes with a white man. She's all right, though, not like you.'

David raised his eyebrows. 'Whatever have I done now, Grandpa?'

'You're trying to steal the gold from

41

me, to bail out this ranch and keep your pa in whiskey. Well you can try to track an old Apache, but you won't get far. Noticed the glint from the glass in your spectacles and saw you off pretty quick, didn't I?'

David laughed. 'I only wear glasses to read, not to follow mad old men around. What a ridiculous story! I've got better things to do. Whoever wanted to follow your trail, it certainly wasn't me.'

Dancing Bird cackled. 'I know what I saw.'

David gave up any further attempt at conversation and went back into the house. A variety of books, ledgers, letters and random pieces of paper were spread out all over the kitchen table. Mark looked up. 'This is it, son. Anything that's got anything to do about money, it's here.'

David frowned. 'I don't suppose you've kept the books up to date since Ma died?'

'I tried, son, but she always did them.

I ain't learned in math, you know that.'

David went over to the sideboard and found his pens and ink where he had left them. 'Take a seat then, Pa, and we'll see what we can do.'

Mark was edging towards the door. 'No, no, going through all that would send me right back to the bottle. I'll head down to the bunkhouse and see what's going on with the hands.'

David looked at the papers in front of him, took his glasses from his pocket and pushed them on. He couldn't help smiling as the numbers came into focus. He always loved figure work. 'Go on then, Pa. But I'll warn you, Grandpa's back.'

★   ★   ★

David was absorbed in his work when Caleb tapped on the doorframe.

He looked up from the books. 'No need to knock,' he said with a tired smile, removing his glasses. 'How can I help you?'

'There's a lady arrived for you, Young Boss.'

David retrieved a handkerchief from his pocket and wiped his fingers, which were ink-stained. 'What does she want?'

'You, sir, she's asking for you. When I say a lady, that's what I mean. I don't mean a woman, or a girl or anything like that, I mean a real lady.'

Intrigued, David followed Caleb outside. When Caleb said 'a lady' he should have realized, but he never thought he would see her again. 'You'd better come in,' he said to her. His voice sounded strained and his legs would not take him down the short flight of steps from the porch to the yard.

'I'll carry the lady's bag,' said Caleb.

David swallowed hard and took a deep breath. 'Yes, yes, leave it in the hall, that'll be all, thank you.' Did that sound better?

'You sure, Young Boss?' Caleb made no secret of the fact he was curious.

'For now, yes, thank you.'

Even though Caleb had taken her small holdall, she too seemed unable to move, and simply looked up at David.

Eventually he managed a step towards the railing of the porch. 'How did you get here?'

She paused and twisted her lips, as if trying to find her voice. 'Train, stage, then I got a lift in a wagon from town, with some prospectors.'

'Prospectors already! I don't believe it. They're wasting their time.'

'You don't know that, Young Boss, your grandpappy's pretty sure — ' interjected Caleb, who was hovering behind David.

'Caleb, please don't let me keep you from your work.'

As Caleb went down the steps he held out his hand to the woman. 'Come along, little lady, up you come.' This seemed enough to give her the power of movement and she finally made it up the steps.

David indicated the front door. 'You'd better come inside. Do you want a drink, or something?'

'I am parched.'

Once in the kitchen he busied himself wiping out a cup and filling it with coffee.

She took it from him with a shy smile. 'What happened to your face?'

'Got into a fight.'

She frowned. 'You? Fighting?'

'It's different here.'

'You still have inky fingers. Just like the first time I met you.'

He ignored her attempt to remind him of better times and looked down at the table. 'I'm trying to sort out Pa's accounts. They're a mess — I think they're beyond me.' Then he turned swiftly, his lips tight with anger. 'Whatever possessed you to come here, Caroline? What risks you took! You can't stay; the ranch is broke, this house is filthy, my father's drunk, my grandpa's started a gold rush, my sister dresses as a man and lives in sin with a drifter — ' He stopped short, because she was smiling at him, amusement in

46

her eyes. 'Oh yes, that's right, laugh, it's hilarious, isn't it. I can't believe you've come all this way to gloat. I'll get one of the hands to take you back to town. You're not welcome here.'

Her smile slipped. She put her cup on the table and moved towards him, but he swiftly stepped back, keeping a distance between them.

'I'm here to see you, David. We parted on such bad terms, I couldn't bear it. I've come to apologize. Believe me, I had no idea of your circumstances until now, but if there's any way I can help — '

'Help a half-breed? As if. Caroline, you are many things, but I never suspected you of lunacy.' He slumped into a chair. 'Just go, please, go.'

She took a seat too, and sat, hands in her lap, staring at the floor. He watched her chest rise and fall slightly as she breathed. He could smell her perfume. Her soft fair hair was pulled into a sensible ponytail, and she wore plain, dark travelling clothes that only accentuated her slim figure and pale, smooth skin. David clenched and unclenched his fists as feelings and memories he had no wish to revive surged through him. The love, the desire, the need to hold her. She may not have been as lax with her morals as his sister, but they had shared some exquisite moments together. Then came the anger, the hatred, and worse than that, the disappointment of her betrayal. He heard footsteps in the hall and Louisa ran in.

'We've got a visitor!' She looked at Caroline who had hastily risen. 'Wow, hello, miss.' She turned to David. 'A friend of yours?'

'Just someone I knew. She's not staying. Get Caleb to take her back to town.' He pushed back his chair and marched out of the room.

'Well, even by his standards that was rude,' exclaimed Louisa.

'I deserve it,' said Caroline, softly. 'You must be David's sister. Pleased to meet you, Miss Merkel.'

'Call me Louisa. And you are?'

'Caroline Fisher, from Vermont.' She held out her hand. 'David never told you about me?'

'Me and Pa aren't much for letter writing. Davy only ever told Ma anything.' Louisa took her hand and squeezed it sympathetically. 'You must really love him to come this far. What's wrong with that man? You're lovely; he should be holding you tight and smothering you with kisses.'

Caroline wrapped her arms around her body and groaned softly. 'I wish. He was handsome in Vermont, but to see him here, so dark, so strong . . . it brought back all the feelings I had for him, and more. I ache for him so much it really hurts.'

For a moment Louisa was speechless. 'Well I'll be . . . ' she muttered at last, briefly wondering if there was something wrong with her and Flynn, since physical pain didn't feature in their relationship. 'This is serious.' She got up and took a bottle and two glasses from the cupboard. 'Here, have this. You need a stiff drink, and so do I.'

Louisa had little difficulty in extracting as much information from Caroline as she wanted, for their visitor was eager to tell her story.

David had worked in her father's bank, at first in a lowly position, but Mr Fisher had noticed his potential and exploited it and David had soon risen to a senior role. He became such a favourite of the family that they had no objection when he began to court their only child.

'I think Father saw him as the son he'd always wanted. Then came that happiest of days. David asked me to marry him, but there was something he had to tell me first, in the strictest confidence, about his mother.'

'Caroline, you don't strike me as stupid, but did it never occur to you he could be half Indian?'

She shook her head. 'No, never. Now I don't know how I could have been so blind, but then, I suppose I just thought he was tanned. Believe me, I wanted nothing more than to be his bride, and was happy to accept his proposal. Then I began to worry, foolishly and irrationally, I know, what effect it might have on our children. So I confided my concerns to my mother. She could not cope with the knowledge I would marry a half-breed and told my father. There was an ugly scene at the bank the next day. I never had a reason to be ashamed of my father, until then.'

Louisa snorted. 'He could at least have sacked Davy in private.'

'Yes,' said Caroline softly.

'So, you've run away from your parents, and hope to make it up with my brother.'

'No, I'm here with a letter from my father begging David's forgiveness. We all missed him so terribly. We realized how hastily we had acted. David is the same man now as he was then. Father would take him back immediately. Plead for me, Louisa, please.'

Louisa topped up their glasses and let

out a long sigh. 'Well I'll be a . . . Well I don't know, but I'll plead for you all right. I can see a problem, though, a big one.'

Caroline looked at her with concern. 'I think you've broken Davy's heart.'

* * *

'I gotta say this,' said Mark to his son, 'since you've been back things have livened up.'

'Don't blame everything on me,' said David.

'I think I gotta blame that beautiful blonde on you. My word, you make a handsome pair.' It was true. While David's good looks were all symmetry and smoothness, Caroline's were quirky. Her hair was fair, but her eyes were dark, her nose was slightly tip tilted and her smile charmingly lopsided. Individually they both turned heads; together they made a compelling couple.

David pulled up his horse. He, his father and the hands were riding out, trying to pull together what was left of the herd. 'We ain't an item, Pa. Oh, Miss Caroline Fisher looks the part, I'll grant you, but she's a snake in the grass. Never trust her.'

Mark looked sceptical. 'She's a good girl, I'd put a stake on it.'

David snorted derisively. 'A judgement made after one meeting when she simpered over you disgracefully: 'Mr Merkel' this, 'Mr Merkel' that.'

Mark smiled. 'She's got good manners to go with those good looks, for sure. And that was some stunt she pulled off, telling her parents she was going to the post office and coming all the way to Arizona instead. Plucky!'

David kicked his horse, who sprang back into life. 'Pa, since Louisa insists that Caroline stays tonight, I'm going round the entire boundary fence. See what I can mend, and see what supplies are needed to fix the rest. That should take me away a few days — she should be gone by then.'

'I already got Tom and Caleb doing

that when we're finished here. Anyway, you can't leave me. We still got to deal with this business of MacPherson and the bank.' Now Mark stopped his horse. 'Hold on now. Caroline's father owns a bank doesn't he, and he's treated you so badly he owes you — '

'Stop right there, Pa, if you so much as whisper that to Caroline I will personally hand the deeds to this ranch to Connor MacPherson.'

'We could do with Lou here, it's a big job,' said Flynn, riding up to them.

'It's good for her to have some female company,' said Mark. 'No doubt they'll be talking weddings.'

Flynn's smile broadened. Mark looked over to David. 'Reckon the pastor could fit another one in easy enough,' he said with a wink.

'Dear God, dear God, dear God,' muttered David, turning his horse around.

★   ★   ★

'Well what an eyeful! I wish all my hands looked like that,' said Mark as they rode back into the yard. Louisa and Caroline were standing by two horses, both women wearing trousers and baggy shirts. Caroline looked particularly fetching. David had to turn away.

'I've never ridden astride before, Mr Merkel,' said Caroline, squinting up at him. 'I'm rather nervous. Lou's going to help me.'

Mark dismounted, gently grasped her shoulders and smiled at her tenderly. 'My name's Mark, remember. Shall I help you up?'

'Give me a minute.'

As David slid from his horse he waved and started to laugh. 'Over here, Grandpa.' He finally looked at Caroline. 'If meeting this old feller doesn't send you rushing back to Vermont I don't know what will.' He pulled Dancing Bird to his side. 'Miss Caroline Fisher, may I introduce you to my esteemed grandfather, Dancing

Bird, of the Apache tribe. He's an Indian, if you hadn't noticed.'

Dancing Bird pursed his lips, this time in a gesture of approval.

Caroline held out her hand. 'I'm honoured to meet you, Mr — um — Bird.'

Dancing Bird cackled happily. 'Now you'll make a fine squaw, yellow hair or not. I can see you in buckskins, with your little brown baby strapped to your back.'

'Oh,' said Caroline. 'That sounds rather exciting. Um, I believe you've started something of a gold rush, Mr Bird.'

Dancing Bird's face clouded with suspicion.

'That's all anyone could talk about on the stage — the gold at Mint River, is it?'

'Creek,' corrected David.

Dancing Bird's wizened features tightened into angry knots. 'Dang blast every last white man from this land. No one's getting my gold.' He ran off towards the stable.

'That went well,' said David, snatching the reins and leading his and his father's horses away.

Caroline leaned forward and pinched the bridge of her nose, as if that would somehow stop her tears. 'I don't think I'll ride after all,' she said to Louisa, swallowing hard. 'How did I manage to make a wonderful man so sour?'

Mark looked at his son's back and shook his head, then returned his gaze to Caroline. 'Ain't you he hates, child. Reckon it's himself.'

4

David had decided to spend the evening in town, reckoning that chewing on a badly cooked steak at the saloon would be preferable to spending the evening in the company of Caroline. In the end, a hard rainstorm, in which only a fool would venture out, caused him to stay on the ranch. He'd moved all the books into the parlour, leaving the women free to do what they wanted in the kitchen, and he continued to try and make some order of his father's financial affairs until he was called to supper.

He certainly fared better for food. Caroline had cooked the chicken and it was delicious. He didn't say as much, but didn't have to as his father and Louise were fulsome in their praise. He could see that they were both completely bewitched by her. He knew how they felt.

'You're a plucky girl, no doubt of it,' said Mark. 'More or less crossing the whole darn country on your own.'

'I've been on a train many times; it was simply longer than any other journey I've done. But the stagecoach and the wagon out here, that was interesting. Especially the wagon. All anyone could talk about was gold, and yet you all seem to think Dancing Bird has made a mistake.'

'Dancing Bird *is* a mistake,' said David, bitterly.

'I thought he was rather charming,' said Caroline. 'And given he must be quite an age, he's very chipper.'

Mark had found a bottle of wine, which he deemed more suitable for the meal than whiskey and he topped up everyone's glasses. 'Doubt if Dancing Bird himself knows how old he is. You've been lucky, though, Caroline, to have such a safe journey. Prospectors can be a rough bunch.'

'The sheriff rode out with us, so I

had no worries. Now he's an interesting man, isn't he?'

David let out an annoyed sigh.

'Got something to say, spit it out, son,' said Mark.

'The man's an idiot,' said David.

'In your present mood you think everyone a fool,' said Mark.

'Ignore him, Caroline,' said Louisa. 'Now what could possibly be interesting about the sheriff?'

'Him being a jailbird. He was telling us how he'd fallen into bad ways as a young man and gone to prison, a place called Yuma, is that right?'

'La Bute in Yuma!' exclaimed Louisa.

'Best place for him,' said David.

Caroline continued. 'When he was released a kindly man from hereabouts, a Mr Mac somebody or other, set him up as the sheriff and made sure he kept on the narrow path. Isn't that heart-warming?'

'Connor MacPherson,' said Mark. 'He's our neighbour. He intends to get his hands on this ranch by any means.

If he shows kindness there's some self-serving reason behind it.'

'Oh, not so heart-warming then,' conceded Caroline.

David pushed his empty plate away and stood up. 'Thank you, Caroline, that was a good meal.'

She reached into her bag and pulled out an envelope. 'This is a letter from my father — '

'No,' said David.

'Take it, son,' said Mark. 'It's up to you if you read it or not.'

David snatched it from her and left the room.

'I think I had better go home,' Caroline said sadly. 'I'd hoped to make things better, but it's not working, is it.'

'Wish you'd stay a while,' said Mark. 'You've come an awful long way just to turn around. And if you keep cooking like this you'll more than earn your keep.'

'I agree,' said Louisa. 'Flynn and I are getting married in three weeks; I'd love you to be there.'

Mark had a sudden thought. 'You should let your parents know where you are.'

'I already have. I got Sheriff la Bute to wire them from his jailhouse.'

'So brave, and all over a man so unworthy,' said Louisa.

'Only because I have made him that way,' said Caroline.

★   ★   ★

The light from the oil lamps was too dim for David's tired eyes to continue perusing the accounts so he retired to his bedroom. He sat on the edge of his bed twisting the envelope round and round, and then, despite his previous protestations he put on his glasses, held the letter close to the candle and opened it.

Dearest David,
How dare I use such familiar terms when I have behaved so badly towards you? I have no mitigation

for my handling of the situation, save that of shock. None of us took you for anything other than a regular American, which, of course, is exactly what you are.

After my anger subsided I set to thinking hard about the situation. Why did the fact that your mother was an Indian upset us all so dreadfully? We stand in church every Sunday, we know we are all equal in the sight of God. All sinners in the sight of the Lord, myself especially. And yet prejudice rose up her ugly head and took possession of me. Are you a different person from the man I have always trusted and liked, a man I fervently wished would take my daughter's hand? No, sir, you are the same, the very same. Are you different from the David who so competently and conscientiously ran my business? No, sir, you are not, you are the very same. All I can do is most humbly ask for your forgiveness. *Please come back to us. Your job still awaits you, and fear not, I will smooth your return, you will find no prejudice against you at my bank. And please, I beg of you, come back to Caroline. If you can never bear to see myself or my wife again, so be it, but please, please put the light back into our darling daughter's eyes.*

God bless you

Horace Fisher

David put the letter and his glasses on the bedside table, kicked off his boots and lay back on the bed. His movement disturbed the candle flame, sending distorted shadows about the room. It was a good letter, written by a man who, until that last day, he had always thought of as decent. How much pressure had Caroline put on him to write it, he wondered. It didn't matter, though. It didn't change anything. All the things Horace had said to him on that hateful day at the bank, though they were inspired by fear and prejudice were, nevertheless, true. He could never return.

* * *

The storm was no more than a memory as David left the house the next morning. He saw dust on the horizon and before long their visitors had arrived.

David held MacPherson's horse as he dismounted. Paulie leapt off his, while the other couple of men with them remained mounted.

'You here for any reason?' asked David.

'To see your pa. I heard he's feeling better.'

'He's been off the bottle for a couple of days if that's what you mean.'

'Thought now might be the time to settle a bit of outstanding business between us.'

David scowled. 'The business where your bank lent money to my sister, a minor, at an exorbitant rate of interest?'

'I'll speak to your pa.' MacPherson pushed past him but stopped as he saw Caroline and Mark coming down the steps towards them. 'Well, well, heard you had a visitor.' He raised his hat. 'I'm Connor MacPherson, pleased to meet you, miss.'

She held out her hand. 'Ah, the man who saved Sheriff la Bute from the error of his ways. I'm Caroline Fisher from Waverley, Vermont, daughter of Horace Fisher, owner of the First Bank of Waverley.'

MacPherson raised an eyebrow at the word 'bank', then shook her hand with a simpering smile dripping off his lips.

David felt anxious. Why had she mentioned that, what was she up to? He guessed, as women cannot keep a secret, Louisa had told her of their financial problems.

'Connor, would you care to step inside?' said Mark.

David grabbed Caroline's arm and squeezed it hard. 'Whatever you're planning forget it. Go and pack your bag. When we're finished here I'm going to personally see you on the stage to Carlyle.'

She tried to pull away from him. 'That hurts! Stop it! My father could help you out of this situation. God knows, David, he owes you. Take me into town by all means, so I can wire him to send over a banker's draft.'

David tugged harder. 'I want nothing and will take nothing from either you or your family! Never, ever. You are leaving today, understood? Now let me go to Pa. I don't want MacPherson befuddling him.'

She looked at him running up the steps, and rubbed her arm. Why, how, could she still love him?

*   *   *

MacPherson tried to shut the parlour door in David's face.

'Let him in,' said Mark. 'David deals with my business. I've no objection if

67

you want Paulie with you.'

'I'll leave that sop with the women,' said MacPherson, letting David through.

Nobody sat down, even though Mark indicated the chairs.

MacPherson pulled a piece of paper from his pocket and handed it to Mark. 'That's it, my final demand. To be paid in full by the end of the month, or else I'll be along with my boys to take possession.' He paused. 'Listen, Merkel, we've known each other long enough. We were the first to make a claim in this valley after all. Why put yourself through more suffering? You ain't going to make the payment, we all know that. You've been a damn fool and you've had bad luck — no business can survive both those blows. Pack up and go and I'll write off half the debt. How about that? I'd say that was a fair and decent offer.'

Mark rubbed his chin. 'You don't know I won't pay in full.'

David breathed hard. 'Have you been talking to Caroline?'

'Girl talks a lot of sense.'

MacPherson began to look a little uneasy.

'You ain't taking nothing from her,' snapped David under his breath, then he looked back to MacPherson. 'Before we go any further I'd still like to know how your bank lent money to my sister.'

MacPherson shrugged. 'We didn't, everything was signed by your pa; check the papers, son.'

'Signed by a man everyone knew was out of his wits with grief and liquor.'

MacPherson smiled a weak, pious smile. 'He signed. It's not for my bank manager to judge a man's state of mind, is it?'

'All the negotiations were done with my sister, who was a girl of eighteen at the time. The rate of interest is obscenely high, my father would certainly never have agreed to that.'

'It's all signed, Davy, no getting away from it. Your pa signed the agreement.'

Caroline was still rubbing her arm when Paulie sidled up to her. 'You can ask me how I got two black eyes and a fat nose if you want.'

'I wouldn't have mentioned it,' she said with a smile, 'but do tell me if you want to.'

'My face ended up on the end of Davy Merkel's fist.'

She took a deep breath. 'He said he'd been fighting.' She paused. 'May I ask why?'

'Oh, it wasn't the truth of what I said to him, reckon it was the way that I said it. We've been friends for years, and we still rile each other.'

'The David in Arizona is very different to the David I knew in Vermont. Back home he was quiet and respectful. Here he's bad-tempered, fights, has a different accent and says 'ain't'.'

Paulie laughed. 'Well, 'ain't' ain't so bad. Have you looked around the ranch much?'

'No, I haven't even seen a cow yet.'

He laughed. 'They ain't milk cows, ma'am, they're steers. Come on, I'll walk you down to the bunkhouse and around the barns and stables if you like.'

'Thank you. You know the ranch, then?'

'Sure, my dad and Mr Merkel were good friends once. We'd come round of an evening sometimes, have some food and a bit of a hoe-down. Yeah, we was all good friends. I had a partiality for Louisa a few years ago, but Pa put a stop to it on account of her ma and that.'

Caroline's sigh was heartfelt as she followed him.

★   ★   ★

Things in the parlour were getting heated. Mark was trying to play peacemaker, wondering if all the effort was worth it and wishing he'd never left his whiskey oblivion. David spoke a lot of sense, and morally he was always right, whilst MacPherson could always fall back on legalities and procedure. The frustration was getting too much for David's temper. Then they all stopped, as a terrified scream rent the air.

'Caroline!' cried David, throwing down the papers he was holding and dashing out of the room so swiftly he almost knocked over Louisa, who'd been listening at the door.

★ ★ ★

Outside David saw MacPherson's mounted men heading down to the stables. He ran, his heart pounding, from fear and effort. She was standing outside the stable, Paulie's arms were around her and he could hear her sobs. He snatched her from him and held her close, his hand smoothing her hair. 'What happened? What's happened?'

She raised her face, which she had buried in his chest, tears poured from her eyes and she looked pale and pinched. 'I thought it was just a pile of old clothes,' she sobbed and he wrapped his arms around her as tightly as he possibly could. 'Caro, Caro, I'm here, I'm here,' he whispered.

Paulie looked at him. He too, was ashen. 'It's your grandpa, Davy, I'm so sorry.'

'Grandpa?' David took a moment to register. 'Dead?'

Paulie nodded. 'I'm sorry. Caroline found him. Not just dead, though.' His voice dropped to a whisper. 'His throat's been cut from ear to ear.'

It was all David could do to keep a hold of Caroline, as his stomach churned and his legs almost buckled. He closed his eyes and breathed hard. His strength returned, though he did not know what had upset him most, the brutal killing of his grandfather, or the fact that Caroline had found him and been subjected to such a gruesome sight.

Louisa, red-faced and breathless, was tugging on his sleeve. David looked at

73

Paulie, who repeated what he had said. He held her steady as she trembled. 'Davy,' she said, looking at her brother, 'what's going on?'

David could see his father and MacPherson coming down the hill, and could hear voices, of the hands and MacPherson's men, in the stable and outside. He had to do something. He gently disentangled himself from Caroline. 'I need to see him,' he said. 'Paulie, take the women to the house.'

Caroline looked up at him, pleadingly, but with an almost imperceptible nod, which let him know she understood what he had to do.

Then he took a deep breath and went into the gloom.

5

It was exactly as Caroline had described it. Alongside one of the mangers lay what appeared to be a pile of old clothes. Only when close up could David discern that inside the rags was the emaciated body of Dancing Bird. His throat had been so deeply cut he was almost decapitated, resulting in his head being tilted at a totally unnatural angle; his eyes were wide and staring, the mouth set in a wide grimace, the tongue lolling. David sank down onto his haunches. Poor Caroline. It was a shocking enough find for anyone, but for a girl from such a sheltered background, the horror must have been magnified.

Tom Sackler was already there. He placed a hand on David's shoulder, and let out a juddering breath. 'This ain't right, Young Boss.'

David pulled himself upright. 'Damn right it ain't, Tom.'

Tom shrugged. 'I heard the young lady scream like she was being murdered herself and rushed over as fast as I could. Never thought I'd find something like this. I mean, he was an old man. Why do this to a harmless old man?'

David shook his head. He wouldn't necessarily ever have described Dancing Bird as harmless, but now he was dead no one would have a bad word to say about him. He heard his father breathing heavily behind him.

'Dear God,' said Mark. 'He's been killed!' He knelt down and tried to reposition the corpse's head into a more natural angle.

'Leave it, Pa,' said David. 'We need the sheriff.'

'I'll saddle up and get him,' said Tom, evidently relieved to have something to do.

'I'd be grateful,' said David. 'And while you're in town maybe the doctor should come out and see Caroline, she must be suffering from complete shock. Pa, we'd best move out the remaining horses and get the door sealed.'

Mark was looking confused. 'How's that going to help? Old man's dead, we need the undertaker.'

'Before anything is moved we need to look and see if the killer has left any clues.'

'Oh, I suppose so. I'll move the horses.'

*   *   *

Back at the house Caroline insisted she had no need of a doctor. Paulie had found some brandy and both the women sat at the kitchen table, sipping the drink and talking quietly. David indicated to Paulie that he wanted to speak to him alone so they retired to the parlour. David closed the door behind him.

'There ain't much to tell, Davy,' said Paulie. 'I offered to walk Miss Fisher around the ranch. We went down to the bunkhouse and had a talk with the hands, then Miss Fisher said something about liking horses, so I said I'd introduce her to those in the stable. We didn't notice anything at first, she was fussing one of the mares, then she said 'Look, someone's left some clothes.' She went to look at the pile and then, well, Davy, you know the rest. I'm mighty sorry about your grand-pappy, mighty sorry.'

David twisted his lips. 'He was an awkward old cuss, I know, but to have his head nearly cut off . . . It makes no sense. He's stone cold, though, so he must have been dead a while. I'll ask around and find out who saw him last.'

Paulie nodded. 'One thing, I don't know if you noticed, the dapple grey gelding was saddled.'

'That was Grandpa's horse,' confirmed David. 'So it looks like he was about to leave.'

★   ★   ★

Mark had put the horses in the barn, and was unsaddling Dancing Bird's grey.

'What was he taking with him?' muttered David, opening the flaps of the saddlebags to reveal a few hard biscuits, a bag of tobacco and a tin cup. Over the pommel of the saddle hung a length of rope with a grappling hook attached. David frowned. 'Where's his pan and stuff for prospecting?'

'Doubt if he ever did find gold. Who knows what he was up to, mad mischief of some sort.' Mark was silent for a while. 'I'll miss the old feller. Odd though he was, I'll miss him.'

David was surprised to hear a suppressed sob emanating from his father's throat.

'Even after he was so cruel to you and Ma, when you first married?'

'Doesn't seem to matter now.'

'Grandpa was killed on our land, Pa, so I think we got to accept the fact it could have been one of us who did it.'

Mark snorted. 'What! One of the

family? The hands? Never, Davy, you got that one wrong. I don't know how Dancing Bird got to die on River Bow land, but sure as hell none of us did it.'

* * *

Louisa had sent Caroline, protesting, to her bed. 'Go to her, Davy. She's been very brave, but having your arms around her will be the best comfort.'

He squinted at her. 'That ain't going to happen.'

'But, I saw you, holding her so tight! Don't try and tell me you don't love that girl. You'd die for her, I could tell.'

'I ain't never said I don't love her. I ain't going to be holding her, that's all.'

Her expression was almost one of distaste. 'What has made you so cruel?'

He ignored her. 'I need to speak to Caroline, though. She might have noticed something. Do you think she's up to it?'

'I'm sure she is.'

'You'd best come upstairs with me, then.'

★ ★ ★

Caroline smiled broadly when she saw them enter the room. A smile that soon died as she realized there would be no fondness from David. She shuddered when he asked her the question.

'Don't answer if it's too painful,' said Louisa, sitting by her.

'It's important, I know that. It's just how Paulie will have told you. I was petting the horses and then I saw the clothes. I reached down, I was going to pick them up and then I saw . . . then I saw . . . Those eyes, staring, staring . . . '

David swallowed hard. 'And you saw no one else in the stable?'

She shook her head. 'No, the door was closed; Paulie had to push it open. Compared to the glare of the sun it was dark inside. It took a few moments for my eyes to adjust, but I'm sure I would have noticed if there'd been anyone there.'

'And only the grey horse was saddled.'

'Yes, that's right. We were just commenting on that when I saw the clothes.'

A slight knock on the door heralded the arrival of the doctor, and David took his leave, relieved that he was away from her just when the need to hold and comfort her was becoming unbearable.

★ ★ ★

Sheriff la Bute was in the stable.

'It's barbaric,' David heard him say. He turned to look at David. 'How's the lady doing?'

'She's brave and strong,' said David. 'What do you think, Sheriff?'

La Bute looked as if he'd never had an original thought in his life. 'Mr MacPherson's not said anything,' he said by way of reply.

David bit his lip in frustration, and then winced at the pain he caused himself. 'You do plan to investigate don't you?'

If la Bute heard or understood the sarcasm in David's tone, he showed no sign, and he was spared any response by the arrival of his mentor.

'So, any clues, Layton?' asked MacPherson.

'Do you think there will be any, Mr MacPherson?'

'I expect so. Was your grandpa alone in the stable, David?'

'As far as we know. There were also three horses in there. One of them belonged to my grandfather and was saddled as if he was ready to go.'

'Back to Mint Creek to find his gold, do you think?' asked la Bute.

'That's what he said he was doing.'

The sheriff was quiet for a moment, then he spoke. 'I think out of decency we should move the body. Have you got anywhere cool?'

David nodded and left the stable to

find something that could be used as a stretcher. He and Mark came back with a length of wood, which would do the trick, and, with David tenderly cradling the old man's head, they nudged him onto it. La Bute bent down and picked up something from under the body. It was a red neckerchief. 'Did this belong to the deceased?' he asked.

Neither David nor Mark knew.

'Bring everyone, except the ladies, to the bunkhouse,' said la Bute, his confidence increasing.

★ ★ ★

La Bute held up the neckerchief. 'Does this belong to anyone here, or does anyone know who it belongs to?'

Caleb raised his arm. 'It's mine, sir,' he said. 'I've been looking for that.'

'It was found under the body of Dancing Bird.'

'Must have dropped it in the stable,' said Caleb.

La Bute snatched back the scarf. 'This is evidence,' he snapped. 'Now, everyone who has a knife, put it on the table.'

The hands, one of MacPherson's men and Mark all obeyed. The sheriff picked them up. He held Caleb's up in front of him. 'There's blood on this blade, boy.'

Caleb seemed unconcerned. 'We had to shoot one of the steers, broken leg. I've been butchering it. It's in the cold room at the back of the kitchen if you want to check.'

'That ain't good enough,' said la Bute. 'Your neckerchief under the body, blood on your knife, you killed the old man, didn't you?'

Caleb took a step back, his eyes widening as the implications of what the sheriff was saying hit him. 'No, sir! No, sir! I ain't never killed nobody, never, sir. I didn't kill Dancing Bird, I liked the old feller.' He stared at Mark. 'I didn't do it, Boss, I swear.'

''Course you didn't,' said Mark. 'No

one on this ranch would hurt Dancing Bird, Sheriff. You're looking in the wrong place. You need to be looking for some drifter or prospector or something. We're like family here; we look out for each other.'

La Bute unhooked his handcuffs from his belt. 'All the evidence says otherwise.'

'Coincidences,' said Mark.

David frowned. Of all the people at the ranch, gentle, straightforward, honest Caleb would not be one of his suspects.

'Young Boss,' pleaded Caleb, 'I'd never hurt your grand-pappy, you gotta believe me.'

'I do,' said David. 'You're jumping to a conclusion based on very little evidence, Sheriff. I'll stand as a character reference for Caleb. He's no murderer.'

'Sheriff can't go against the evidence,' said MacPherson. 'Cuff him and take him back to the jail, Layton. Good work.'

David pulled the front of MacPherson's jacket and pushed his face close to the older man's. 'You ain't the law, Connor. You ain't the law, and you ain't above it, either. You gotta leave this to the proper authorities.'

'Which is me,' said la Bute, deftly attaching the cuffs to Caleb.

'You ain't no proper law man, you're one of MacPherson's hands!' exclaimed David, as he pushed MacPherson away from him so hard he staggered and almost fell onto the table. His men rushed over and grabbed David's arms, but he threw them off and pulled his gun. 'Leave this ranch now,' he snarled. 'You ain't welcome here, none of you are.'

MacPherson tugged his jacket straight and regained some of his composure. 'I'll overlook this on account of your grieving, David. I'll say good day to you, Merkel, and my condolences.' He nodded to Mark.

La Bute had pulled his gun too. 'Caleb is under arrest. Anyone tries to stop me taking him to town will be arrested too.' He looked at Caleb. 'You understand that, boy? You've been arrested for murder and the next marshal comes by you'll be taken to Carlyle to stand trial, and be found guilty.'

Caleb was still protesting as the sheriff pulled him from the bunkhouse, despite the pleas of the hands. David holstered his weapon and ran after MacPherson, who was already outside and heading towards his horse.

'You're a bad man, Connor,' he called after him.

MacPherson turned round. Paulie was at David's side now. 'Steady, old friend,' he whispered. 'Dad will destroy you, you know.'

'He will not,' said David between clenched teeth. 'Connor MacPherson, you need to be brought down to your true level. You're just a rich rancher. You don't own the town, you don't own the law and you sure as hell don't own this ranch. The only way you'll ever come back on this land is by walking over the corpses of me and my pa. Now go!'

MacPherson pulled himself onto his horse. 'You're a hot-head half-breed, David Merkel and you won't ever amount to anything. You're worthless and always have been.' He swung round his mount and galloped off.

'He'll calm down,' said Paulie.

'You go too,' said David, turning his back on him. He went over to Caleb, who was being pushed onto a horse by the sheriff.

'It's all right, Young Boss,' Caleb said. 'I'm happy to stand trial. I didn't do nothing. The judge can't find me guilty if I'm innocent, can he?'

David breathed heavily, but made no comment. Why break the man's faith in justice? 'Be strong, Caleb,' he said. 'I'll find out what really happened.' He turned to the sheriff. 'La Bute, if I discover your prisoner has been mis-treated in any way, I'll scalp you, alive, personally and with pleasure. You keep him well fed and comfortable, eh?'

'He's guilty,' said la Bute, swinging into the saddle, 'but I'm not cruel. I'll keep him well enough to stand trial, don't you doubt it.'

★   ★   ★

Louisa was angry when she heard what had happened. 'You gotta stop it, Davy!' she exclaimed. 'Pa we can't let Caleb hang!'

Mark sighed and poured himself a whiskey.

'Pa, that ain't going to help,' warned David. 'You gotta stay sober and keep things going here while I take Grandpa back to the Apache.'

6

After three days Mark was about to saddle up his horse and ride off to Indian territory when David returned.

'I was getting worried, son. Any trouble?' he said, his relieved smile splitting his face.

David shook his head. 'I found the Apache to be decent folks. They made sure Grandpa got sent on his way in the manner he would have wanted.' He squinted his eyes as he observed a horse tied to the hitching rail outside the ranch house. 'What's that you've got on Shadow?' he asked.

'Side-saddle. Paulie MacPherson brought it over for Caroline.'

'She's still here, then.'

'She's been working hard, Davy, taking down statements from all of us, hoping to get some evidence to clear Caleb.'

David scowled. 'That ain't her business. And Shadow's our fastest and most difficult horse. She ain't going to be riding him.'

Mark laughed. 'Too late, son.'

David's scowl deepened. 'Never mind, I'll sort her out later. Give me half an hour to wash up and get some things sorted, then get all the men in the bunkhouse.'

* * *

David came into the room carrying some papers. He laid a large sheet out on the table. 'Gather round,' he said. 'I've been doing a lot of thinking while I've been gone.'

Obediently, they all gathered around the table.

'Here's the map Pa had when he first made claim to the ranch. I've marked some other things on it. Now here's us.' He pointed. 'There's Carlyle, which we know is fourteen hours and fifteen minutes away by stage.'

'Oh no, you ain't thinking on putting the steers on the stage are you?' scoffed Flynn.

David's sigh was one of irritation. 'Thank you for that suggestion,' he said. 'My plan's going to look pretty dull by comparison. Now, the stage takes this route.' He traced his finger along the paper. 'It goes up through the hills and even with an experienced driver, some of those mountain passes are pretty scary.'

'You couldn't do it with a herd, Young Boss,' said Tom.

'I agree,' said David. 'But given we haven't got time to get to Blackwater, our only alternative is Carlyle. The herd's the only asset this ranch's got. They're all steers, we can't breed with them. All we can do is sell them for meat.'

Mark groaned and put his head in his hands. 'I should've thought of this; I've known about the loan for months. We could easily have taken the herd to Blackwater.'

'No point going on about what you should've done, Pa. For numerous reasons you didn't, now I'm trying to make the best of the situation.'

'But you can't drive cows to Carlyle,' said Tom. 'You'd never get them across the desert.'

Caroline saw David's jaw tighten; he was making a monumental effort to keep his temper.

'Unless we do it this way,' he said, when he had eventually regained control. Once again he traced a route with his finger. 'We go along the river up to here, where we will have to cross part of the desert, I admit. We fill up as many barrels as we can for us and our horses, then overnight, we push across the desert, towards the canyon and Mint Creek Falls. We should get there the following day and there'll be plenty of water. We follow the creek, as far as here.' He tapped the map. 'I reckon that's another three days' driving. Then across the second part of the desert. Once again, if we do it by night it should be easier on the animals. And there we are at Carlyle.'

Nobody spoke.

David continued. 'Apart from crossing the desert the main difficulty will be getting the herd through the canyon at Mint Creek Falls. It's very narrow and they're going to bunch, so we need to be real good drivers, but then, most of us are.'

'You've put a good deal of thought into this, Young Boss,' said Tom, 'and we all know why you've done it, but I can't see it working. The herd ain't in good condition — we stand to lose a lot.'

'I've figured that in,' said David. 'As long as we can sell for minimum price we're likely to get, even if we lose a third, we'll make just enough to pay off MacPherson.'

'Hmm,' said Tom. 'There's just the other problem, then.'

'Go on, Tom.'

'Once we get to Mint Creek Falls most of the rest of the drive goes plum through Indian country.'

'Yes, it does. But I'm an Indian, why would that bother me?'

'You think they'll let us through?'

'Sure they will.' David allowed himself a brief smile.

'You've spoken to them about this, haven't you?' said Caroline.

David nodded. 'I don't think they'd be too happy if someone else did it, or too often, but just this once, they'll be fine about it, me being a relative and all.'

Mark, who had been leaning over the table, studying the map intently, stood up and stretched his back. 'All right, son, let's say it all goes to plan, which nothing ever does, and we get to Carlyle and sell the herd. What then?'

'Once we've got the banker's draft you hightail it to Clearwater and pay off what we owe. What I'd like to do is go to one of the reputable banks in Carlyle and take out a proper loan, with affordable interest payable over three years, and use that to buy some young heifers and a few bulls, and breed ourselves a new herd.' He opened out the second piece of paper. 'I've written out my business plan. It makes sense. When I worked in a bank,' he couldn't help himself shooting a sharp look at Caroline, 'I would have lent money on the strength of these proposals.'

Mark let out a long breath. 'It would be like starting all over again.'

'Yes,' said David. 'Maybe that's what we all need. It ain't going to be a long drive, but it'll be a hard one. We all need to go.' He looked at his sister. 'I'd have liked to leave you behind, but we really do need every hand. The milk cow's nearly dry so we may as well take her and you'll have to let the chickens go, but they ain't laying much anyway.'

'I don't mind staying and looking after the house, or helping with the drive, whatever,' said Caroline.

'You ain't going to be here,' said David under his breath.

'Young Boss,' said Tom. 'I'm willing to give it a go.'

'You can count me and Olly in,' said Stumpy.

'You know I think you're mad,' said Flynn, 'but let's do it. How good it would be to see that greedy smile wiped off of MacPherson's face once and for all. And if we can do it legal, decent and honest, then the victory will be all the sweeter knowing there's no way he can get back at us. Hell, what've got to lose?'

'The ranch,' muttered David.

'That's settled then,' said Mark with a cautious smile. 'What about those steaks you promised, Olly?'

Caroline turned to David. 'I think you've been brilliant,' she couldn't help saying, her eyes sparkling with admiration for him. 'I've got an idea too. There's no need to go borrowing off some strange bank. You say you've made a good plan — Daddy's bank will invest. It won't be charity or anything, simply straightforward business. Even you can't quibble about that and at least you'd be dealing with someone you know you can trust.'

David gripped Caroline's arm. 'Out-side, now,' he snapped.

⋆   ⋆   ⋆

They stood outside the bunkhouse, illuminated by the hurricane lamp that hung from a bracket on the wall. The air was warm, and the ceaseless chirping of the cicadas serenaded them.

'I'm taking you back to Clearwater Springs tomorrow,' said David. 'I believe Pastor Sims and his wife run a decent boarding house; you can stay there until the next stage.'

'I meant it when I said I'd help with the cattle drive,' said Caroline.

'You'd be no help, believe me.'

'I suppose if I do go back at least I can talk directly to Daddy. You just need to wire me where you are and I can tell Daddy to wire the banker's draft to you.'

He gripped both her arms and shook

her slightly. 'What makes you think I would borrow a bent cent from your 'daddy'? He's not a man I trust. He's a man who denounced me, in front of all my former colleagues, as the son of a squaw. Now how do you think that made me feel?'

'He's apologized for that,' she spat breathlessly. 'Stop this, David, this isn't like you.'

'You don't know me at all.'

'I do, I thought I did. Please, David, let me help. You have no idea how sorry Daddy is. In matters of business, if nothing else, he is trustworthy, and in your heart of hearts, you know that. Let him, let us, make amends.'

'I don't want you to make amends. I want you to go. After tomorrow I don't ever want to see you again. Never, ever. This has got nothing to do with you. You might have tried to poke your nose into our business, but you'll never belong here.' He pushed her away.

She sniffed loudly in the darkness. 'I

know we all hurt you badly, so very badly. Can you never bring yourself to forgive us, forgive me?'

'By Christ, Caroline, can't you understand? There is and never was anything to forgive. Every word your pa spoke was God's honest truth. Now you go up to the house and pack your bag. You'll find something to eat up there; it'll be better than the stuff Olly serves. We'll be leaving for town at first light tomorrow. Make sure you're ready or I'll load you onto the wagon in your nightgown.' He turned and went back into the bunkhouse, giving the door a solid slam behind him.

★ ★ ★

After they'd eaten David and the hands huddled together and began to make their plans. Mark excused himself from the bunkhouse on the pretence of getting his pipe. Once up at the house he checked there was a light on in

Caroline's room before he knocked on the door.

She opened it. 'Mr Merkel, how can I help?'

'My name's still Mark.' He held up a bottle and two glasses. 'I know I can use a drink, thought maybe you could too.'

She hesitated. 'I don't think David would approve,' she said.

Mark smiled broadly. 'All the more reason to do it, then. Don't worry, I don't aim to drink myself stupid. I'd like to talk to you, and I'd find it more relaxing with a glass in my hand, that's all. I'll be in the parlour.'

A few minutes later she joined him, and took a sip from the whiskey he'd poured.

'Would you prefer wine?' he asked. 'I may have a bottle of something else, I could have a look.'

'No, Mark, this will do fine.' She raised her glass and they toasted each other.

'So he's finally persuaded you to go,' said Mark after a short silence. 'All things considered he may be right, but I'm not happy.'

'I think you've got a big enough job without having to train up a greenhorn cowgirl on a side-saddle. Do you think David's plan will work?'

Mark shrugged. 'Maybe. Let's hope. Now, tell me, Caroline, what did he say to persuade you to leave? I'll remind you that this is my ranch, and you're my welcome guest for as long as you like.'

She paused. 'You love him so much don't you? And he you. You're good for each other.'

'What cruel thing did he say?'

'I don't think I realized until tonight that David is so badly hurt by what happened, that no matter what apologies are made, no matter how much I try to atone, nothing can be done to repair the damage.'

Mark leaned back in his chair and took a sip of his drink. 'What exactly did happen?'

Caroline sighed a long juddering

sigh and took another tot before she spoke. 'Daddy called everyone from the bank together for an announcement. David thought it was to tell them that we were engaged. But it wasn't. Daddy denounced him in the vilest terms as a half-breed, a liar and a deceiver. Then he went on to say how he had tried to seduce me. That was never true. David was always honourable. Then Daddy said that if we married I would have been condemned to a half-life, living with a half-breed. People would point and disapprove and our children would have no future.' She stopped abruptly and finished the whiskey in her glass. 'It was horrible, horrible. David is right, we don't deserve to be forgiven. I shouldn't even have tried to make things right.'

Mark leaned forward and refilled both their glasses. 'There's a lot of truth in what your pa said. It's hard work and often heartbreaking to be married to someone different. My Mary was never accepted, and that hurt me. Oh, some people were polite to her face, but you never knew what they whispered behind their hands. Others simply spat at her. Once I took her to Carlyle so she could get herself some nice clothes and stuff. We went to the church there. The pastor made it quite clear after the service he didn't expect her to attend again.'

Caroline frowned and shook her head. 'That's so unchristian.'

'It's the way it is. And your pa got it right; it ain't fair on the children. Ours knew they were different from an early age. We couldn't protect them for long. They knew they and their ma were despised. It made Louisa ornery and tough; Davy, well he's a deep one, who knows what damage is done. And it affects their chances, it's true. If Davy hadn't been a breed he'd still be working at the bank and you'd be planning your trousseau.' He fiddled awkwardly with his glass for a moment. 'So, I suppose I was selfish to marry my Mary and to give her children. But let me tell you something, Caroline, I don't regret it for one single solitary moment. To find a soulmate in life is the most precious, priceless thing you can have. There's no amount of money or success that can come anywhere near. And we made good children. If the world can't see that, it's the world that's wrong.' He paused. 'But the world is wrong a lot of the time, and it don't change nothing just saying so.' He stopped again and breathed deeply. 'I don't know what I'm trying to say, Caroline. I suppose I like you, and I'm finding it damn hard to accept you ain't going to be my daughter-in-law.'

Tears were pouring from her eyes. Mark Merkel might look to the rest of the world like an ignorant cow man from an alien territory, but he was as sensitive, thoughtful and understanding as any fancy-dressed 'gentleman' from the East.

He stood up. 'Sorry I made you cry,

child, that wasn't my intention. We'll say our goodbyes in the morning.'

She rushed over to him and gripped him tightly. 'I shall miss you, I shall miss you all so much,' she sobbed.

7

Caroline watched David's strong brown hands grip the reins as he gee'd up the horses pulling the wagon. He had been particularly surly towards her that morning. If this was to be their last journey together she wished it could be more amicable.

'Did you read the statements I took from the hands?' she said to break the ill-tempered silence.

'Didn't help, but thank you.'

'I had a very pleasant and informative talk with your father last night.'

'Good for you.'

'I think your pa thinks you're determined to be rid of me to save me from the prejudice I'll have to face if I'm married to a half-breed.'

David shook the reins and clicked at the horses. 'The man's entitled to his own opinion.'

'Your pa said it was worth it to be married to you mother, even though it seems people in town treated her with somewhat less respect than they should have done.'

David snorted. 'You could put it that way. I don't know what happy memories you carry from your childhood, but I don't suppose they include your ma being spat on by the madam from the Lucky Dollar saloon, to name but one, or the church minister telling her she weren't welcome at service, or your pa being called squaw-man, or you being called 'breed' even by people you think are friends.' He shot her a hurt, angry look.

'No, David, of course I don't have those experiences.'

'And you shouldn't. You won't.'

'We would stand up against these people, show them how wrong they are.'

His mouth twisted angrily. 'Will you do me a favour, Caroline?'

'Of course.'

'I've got a deal of thinking to do. I've got a herd to drive to Carlyle, and I'm on a promise to Caleb to get him out of jail. I'd appreciate it if you kept quiet, while I do some pondering.'

She turned away from him and gazed sightlessly at the parched countryside. But her mind could not be idle for long. Poor Dancing Bird's body still haunted her when no other thoughts intruded. Why would anyone want to kill him? And Louisa had told her that she'd heard his body showed signs of a beating, possibly even torture. She shivered at the thought.

David looked at her. 'You can't be cold.'

'No, someone walked over my grave — your grandpa, actually. You get back to your pondering.'

★   ★   ★

They could hear raised voices inside the jail.

'Those prospectors ain't no business of yours, la Bute,' Connor MacPherson was shouting. 'I pay you to keep the law in *my* town. Leaving Johnny Shand, that in-bred half-wit from the livery stable, in charge of the prisoner ain't good enough.'

'I was trying to nip any trouble in the bud, before they bring it to your town,' said la Bute.

'No you weren't. You've been prospecting while I'm still paying your wages. I know what you're up to.'

David walked in.

'I can't be here all the time, we need a deputy,' la Bute was saying.

'I'll volunteer as a deputy,' said David with a bland smile to MacPherson. 'I'll happily take care of Caleb.' He went over to the cell. 'How's it going, friend?'

'They're feeding me, but the company ain't great,' said Caleb, smiling and waving to Caroline as she approached the bars with a basket.

'Sheriff la Bute,' she said with a

winning smile, 'would you mind opening the door, I've brought Caleb a picnic.'

'Picnic!' spluttered MacPherson. 'The man's due to hang and you bring him a picnic!'

'I didn't realize we'd had the trial already,' said David. 'Don't forget Caleb's no more than a suspect. Damn, I wish I had some learning in law; what you're doing has got to be illegal.'

La Bute was pulling his keys from his belt. 'Mr MacPherson, you sure you don't want to deputize Mr Merkel here? You'll only blame me when the prospectors come to town and trash the place.'

'They ain't going to trash the place, and if you think I'd deputize a breed like Merkel, even if I wasn't in dispute with his pa, you're wrong.'

Caroline snapped round. 'How dare you use such an expression! Apologize immediately.'

MacPherson obviously thought that most amusing, as he chuckled heartily.

'Why, Miss Hoity Toity from Vermont, you sure got a wasp in your petticoats.' He snatched out and pulled David towards him by the collar of his waistcoat. 'You got problems down below, boy? You surely ain't satisfying that woman, are you? She's as prickly as a porcupine. You give her a good seeing to and she'll soon calm down.'

Caroline stamped her foot. 'You really are a most repellent individual, aren't you, Mr MacPherson. It makes me wonder what your problems might be that you behave so appallingly to everyone.'

'Oh, my, my, but you are priceless, my girl.'

'Give Caleb his food and we'll go,' said David.

With a hard look at MacPherson Caroline went into the cell and embraced Caleb warmly. 'At least there's a decent meal here,' she said, putting the basket on the bench, before leaning forward again. 'David will do what he can,' she whispered, 'you know that, but there's been all sorts of trouble at the ranch. He's going to try and drive the herd to Carlyle, so you'll have to be patient and trust us. I'm going to wire my father and get him to send you an attorney.'

Caleb looked surprised and greatly touched. 'Miss, you can't do that for me,' he whispered.

'I can, because it's the right thing to do.'

'I'll take you to the boarding house,' said David, indicating to her that they should leave the jail.

★   ★   ★

'There must be something wrong with MacPherson. He's insane!' she fumed as David pointed the wagon towards the church. He stopped outside and handed her down.

'Do you want me to come inside with you?' he asked.

'No need,' she said, taking her bag from him. Suddenly a lump formed in

114

her throat. 'David,' she croaked, 'I can't believe — '

He jumped back onto the wagon. 'Best I just go,' he said, hauling round the horses.

Resignedly she knocked on the door of the house next to the church.

★ ★ ★

David left the list at the general store and went to the saloon. Paulie, who despite his protestations, did always seem to be there, offered to buy him a beer.

'Make it a whiskey,' said David, his voice hoarse. He wished Paulie hadn't been there as he had no desire to talk to anyone, but then he noticed his friend's face. 'That's not due to me, is it?' he asked, pointing at the bruises and scabs.

'No,' laughed Paulie, handing him the whiskey. 'Dad got annoyed with me.'

David hardly heard what Paulie said

and drank the whiskey; the smooth liquid seemed to soothe the soreness in his throat, which had formed there since he'd said goodbye, or rather hadn't said goodbye, to Caroline.

Paulie looked rueful. 'Don't know what's got into Dad these days. He's always been a strong, ambitious man, but his hatred for your family and you in particular, has become extreme. I just wish he'd let the whole thing about the loan and the ranch die down. He and your pa were friends once; they started up their ranches at the same time, after all.'

'Your pa's got rich and he likes it. Nothing a rich man wants more than more riches.'

'Hmm, maybe you're right. How's Miss Fisher?'

David finished his whiskey. 'Going back to Vermont.'

'That's a pity, Miss Fisher leaving. I like her. I suppose we're just a bit too rough for her. Don't worry about that old saddle, we've got no use for it.'

David headed back for the store. Caroline was sitting in the passenger seat of the wagon and despite himself he felt cheered.

'There's no stage for at least a month,' she explained. 'It fell over or something and the driver got injured and the company's short of money and there's all sorts of other reasons. Anyway, the upshot is, no stage. So I thought as you're going to Carlyle I might as well go with you. I can ride with Olly in the chuck wagon. It makes sense, you must see that.'

He looked away. He didn't want her to see the relief in his eyes. 'Makes no sense to me. You go back and book into the boarding house.'

'For an indefinite period, with obligatory daily Bible readings, prayers and hymn singing, led by sanctimonious Pastor Sims and his wife, who's even worse than he is? No thank you. I'd rather take my chances at the Lucky Dollar.'

'I'll go and pay for my supplies,' he

said, rushing into the store before she could see how broadly he was smiling.

*　★　*

'I'm doing this under protest,' he said as he pulled himself into the driving seat. He'd more or less got his expression under control, but Caroline was no fool. She could see the tension had gone from his face. Pastor Sims' (actually completely unsanctimonious) wife was right. Sometimes men don't know what's best for them. And God will, for sure, forgive a lie when it's necessary to further the right outcome. She just hoped they were well away from Clearwater Springs before he had a chance to speak to anyone else. Before they left, though, she had to show David something.

'Drive slowly past the jail and look at the horse at the hitching rail there,' she said.

He frowned but obeyed. 'One's MacPherson's horse and the other, I'm presuming, is la Bute's.'

'It is, and look what's tied to the saddle.'

'Rope,' said David. 'That's pretty common for these parts.'

'I know that, but look what's attached to the rope. A grappling hook, which is exactly what Dancing Bird was taking when he went prospecting. I saw his horse in the stable, remember?'

David frowned. 'What are you trying to say, Caro?'

'I don't know. I simply thought I'd point it out to you. You're the one doing the thinking after all.'

*　*　*

'Well that's the darndest thing,' said Mark. 'Even when we had trouble with the Apache the stage always ran. Not always on time, but it always ran. Never mind, we've got you back for a few more days, Caroline, which suits me fine.'

Whilst not an experienced liar

Caroline knew better than to compound an untruth so she kept quiet and smiled.

'Now, let me find myself a slip of paper and a pencil,' said Mark. 'You sit down at the table there and I'll show you how we drive a herd.'

'She'll be in the chuck wagon with Olly,' said David.

'Shame to waste her there,' said Mark.

Louisa slipped her arm into David's and led him onto the porch. She pulled him close.

He looked down at her. 'It don't mean nothing, Caroline coming back. It was sensible, that's all. Sooner I get her onto the train back to Vermont, the better. And she can't come to any harm with Olly, which is where she'll be.'

She smiled up at him. 'This morning you were angry, and so very sad. Now, look at you; your eyes sparkle, you look alive again. Admit it, Davy, you can never be content without her.'

He shook her off, roughly. 'What

rubbish you prattle, woman. As soon as we get to Carlyle Miss Fisher is on the next train East. I shall personally take her aboard and be pleased to do so.'

She laughed and shook her head. 'How was Caleb?'

'Bearing up. Damn, we could really use him on this drive.'

She pushed him. 'You're a hard man, David Merkel. Well, you think you are.'

'You'll find out just how hard I am at daybreak tomorrow. You and Caro seem to have some damn fool notion in your minds that this cattle drive's going to be little more than a rather jolly ride in the park with a picnic thrown in. Well it ain't going to be like that, and if by this time tomorrow you ain't begging me to shoot you, I've failed.'

8

The chill of the night was swiftly burning away as the sun rose over the plain.

David had gone to bed with his mind so teeming he doubted he would slumber for a minute. In fact he'd slept soundly and it was the sound of the others getting up that awakened him.

'You're not leading by example, then,' said Louisa with a sarcastic smile as she put his breakfast in front of him.

'Has anyone thought to wake up Caroline?' he asked.

'She's down at the stables already,' said Mark, draining the last of his coffee. 'Which is where I'm going now. See you in a minute, son.'

David gobbled his eggs, pulled on his coat and picked up his saddle roll from the hall and jumped down the steps from the porch. At last he was doing something. Whether it worked or not was another matter, but it was a good feeling to be in action.

It was as if a miniature army was at work in the yard. The chuck wagon had been loaded and most of the horses had been saddled. He saw that Caroline's side-saddle was on Shadow. He considered making some comment about it, but decided it wasn't worth the effort. After a few hours of cattle driving she'd be begging to sit with Olly. He found her in the stable about to lead out Stumpy and Flynn's horses. He stopped in the doorway. She was wearing a loose blouse and a pair of pants he thought may once have belonged to himself. Her hat was pushed firmly onto her head. She looked up from the bridle she was adjusting. 'Good morning,' she said.

He reached into his pocket and retrieved the neckerchief he had put there. 'Here,' he said, holding it out for her. 'It gets pretty dusty on the trail; you'll need to put this round your face.'

'Why thank you,' she said, taking it from him as if he had given her a precious gemstone. 'That was kind.' She tied it round her neck.

'With so few hands I can't afford to have any of you choking on trail dust.'

'I'm riding, by the way. Your pa said he'd keep an eye on me.'

'Pa's got a herd to keep an eye on, you remember that.'

★ ★ ★

Everyone had gathered in the yard.

'Is that everything, men?' called Mark.

There were general grunts of assent.

'Then let's do it.'

They had all mounted when they heard the sound of galloping hoofs and a man shouting.

David squinted into the low sun. 'Two riders,' he said, kicking his horse into a canter to meet them.

Flynn put his hand over his eyes. 'If I'm not mistaken one of them's Caleb.'

'What!' exclaimed Caroline. 'The sheriff must have released him.'

David had reached the riders now and after a brief pause, all three galloped into the yard.

'The other one's Paulie MacPherson,' said Louisa. 'Last thing we want is him telling his pa what we're up to.'

All three horses were now being pulled up. 'Paulie sprung Caleb from jail and he's come to join us,' said David, breathlessly.

'How come, son?' Mark asked Paulie.

'Dad beat me up once too often, Mr Merkel. Decided I'd had about as much as I could take. I reckoned the two things that would rile him most would be breaking his prisoner out and coming to work as a hand for the River Bow.'

'By Jesus, MacPherson will kill us all,' said Flynn under his breath.

'I didn't know what to do, Boss,' said Caleb. 'Young Paulie here got me outta prison on the point of his gun. I don't want to cause you any more trouble.'

'You all going somewhere?' asked Paulie.

David saw no reason not to tell him. 'We're driving the herd to Carlyle. You ready for a hard drive, cowboy?'

Paulie laughed. 'You can't do that, you've got to cross the desert and Indian country!'

'Only way to get to Carlyle.' David raised his hand. 'Come on, follow me!'

With much snorting and with hoofs clattering and Olly's old cart creaking they headed out for the range.

Caleb brought his horse into step beside Shadow. 'Have I done wrong, miss?' he asked Caroline.

'You've escaped from jail,' she said. 'Given that you were wrongly imprisoned, I don't know how much of a crime that is.'

'You didn't get a chance to contact your daddy, I hope.'

'I wired him to send the best attorney he could find to Clearwater Springs.'

Caleb groaned. 'He'll have to be pretty special to get me out of this.'

David rode up to them. 'How'd Paulie get you out?' he asked Caleb.

'Easy. He told la Bute he'd guard me if the sheriff wanted to go back to Mint Creek. The man's been desperate to go up there again. It took very little persuasion to get him to hand the keys to Paulie.'

'I don't know what Mr MacPherson's going to do when he finds out,' said Caroline.

'Reckon he'll need your daddy's attorney,' said Caleb, 'because he's going to murder us all for sure.'

Caroline winced.

David narrowed his eyes. 'You got something to tell me, Miss Fisher? Have you broken your word to me — again?'

'I promised not to tell Daddy about the ranch and I've kept that promise. If I want to ask my father to arrange a legal representative for Caleb, that's between me, Caleb and Daddy.'

Mark cantered up. 'Here's the first of them,' he said, pointing at the cattle.

'Davy, you and Caleb go to the front, Caro, stay with me. Caleb, the plan is to get them to the river.'

'Yes siree, Boss,' said Caleb. He turned back to Caroline and David. 'Reckon everything else got to wait till we get these cows delivered.'

★ ★ ★

Caroline was suddenly aware that she couldn't smell the cattle any more. At first she had found their pungency unpleasant, then it had become bearable and now she had become so used to it she wondered if she would notice fresh air when she was eventually exposed to it. Getting the cattle across the river had been tricky, but it was eventually achieved, although she could tell David was frustrated by how long it took.

She shifted in her saddle.

'You want to ride in the wagon a while?' asked Mark, who, good to his word had kept an eye on her.

128

'No, I'm fine, really. Better than I expected. Back home I go out hunting all day, often at a much faster pace than this, so I should be all right.'

'One day,' said Mark with a smile. 'Maybe it'll get to you after two or three.'

'Doubtless,' she replied.

⋆   ⋆   ⋆

David took a small swig from his water canteen and twisted round in his saddle. The herd were holding together well. He'd feared for the worst as they crossed the river. The regular hands were rusty and the others inexperienced. They'd got them through, though, and the hands were getting back in their stride and the new ones were fast learners. No matter how or why they were there, he was pleased he had Paulie and Caleb, as both were competent. It would have been much more difficult without them. He twisted in the other direction. He could just make out the chuck wagon trundling along at the rear. His sister and Flynn were bringing in some stragglers and Mark and Caroline were keeping their side of the herd in order. As he looked a steer decided he'd make his own way to Carlyle. Without having to be told Caroline had flicked Shadow round and gently pushed the beast back on track. To the other side, though out of view he knew that Paulie and Tom were keeping their portion of the herd under control.

'You happy, Young Boss?' asked Caleb.

David didn't answer immediately. 'I am content, for the moment.'

'I'd forgotten just how good this could be,' said Caleb. 'Ain't nothing ever going to get me back into that prison cell.'

★ ★ ★

After a hard day's driving even Olly's beef stew tasted good, as they sat around their camp-fire, exchanging reminiscences of the day.

'I ain't asked you to shoot me yet,' said Louisa to her brother. 'So I reckon you owe me a dollar.'

'I never mentioned money,' said David. 'And if you ain't pleading for a bullet then I'm not working you hard enough. Driving all night will separate the men from the girls.'

'I'll come back and pick you up off the ground, if I'm feeling generous,' she laughed.

David turned to Olly. 'Pass me that spy glass of yours will you?' Taking the telescope he jumped up onto the seat of the chuck wagon and scanned the horizon. 'Come up here, Pa,' he said, 'we need to work out a few markers. Reckon I can just about make out the canyon.'

Mark climbed up next to him, and they engaged in deep conversation that involved pointing, squinting at the horizon and consultation with the map.

'He's loving this, isn't he,' said Caroline to Louisa. 'Being in charge, planning, organizing.'

'Bossing,' said Louisa, but she was smiling. 'I'll say one thing for my irritating, proud, selfish brother, if anyone can make this drive work, it'll be him.'

★ ★ ★

They began to drive the herd away from the river, and out into the unforgiving waste of the desert. The sun was low in the sky, occasionally burning into their eyes.

Caroline gazed around in awe. 'Everything's changing colour,' she breathed to Mark. 'I don't think I've ever seen anywhere so beautiful.' The distant hills that surrounded them had reddened and become striped with yellow and long deep shadows gouged into the plain.

David rode up to them. 'Probably time to light our lamps,' he said. 'We'll lose the light pretty quickly from now on.' He looked behind him. 'There ain't much of a moon, either.'

'If we have to stop and camp up, so be it,' said Mark.

'I know,' said David. 'But I was hoping to keep to schedule.'

'Let's see how it goes, son,' said Mark.

'Time you joined Olly in the wagon,' David said to Caroline.

'Only if you want to,' Mark said to her. 'You stay with me if you don't.'

'Sort it out between yourselves, then,' snapped David and cantered off.

By one in the morning it was pitch black and no one had any real idea where they were going. Reluctantly David called a halt.

'It's no bad idea, Young Boss,' said Tom. 'We all need a rest. I reckon we'll get light in the sky between four and five. We'll get going then.'

*　*　*

Caroline was awoken by the movement of the chuck wagon. She pulled herself to the front and onto the seat next to Olly. The light, what little of it there was, was grey and flat; gone were the warm colours of the sunset.

'You should have woken me, how long have we been going?'

'Not long at all. Just as well we stopped, though, we were beginning to drift off course.'

'Oh dear. How angry is David?'

Olly chuckled. 'Reckon you've got the measure of him. Everything don't always work like clockwork. The sooner he understands that, the happier he'll be.'

* * *

'Good morning,' said Mark to Caroline as she finally joined him. He waved aside her apologies. 'We'll be fighting each other for the back of that wagon before we're finished with this.'

They plodded on as dawn turned to morning and morning to full daytime, the hot sun burning down relentlessly.

Some of the cows fell in sight of Caroline. She looked to Mark.

'Gotta leave them,' he said with a regretful sigh.

Then the pace seemed to liven a little. Mark stood up in his stirrups and squinted ahead. 'Reckon they can smell water,' he said. 'The canyon should be just over there, between those two outcrops of rock in the distance. Can you see?'

She nodded, pleased to have the protection of David's neckerchief over her nose and mouth.

'Come on you beeves, come on boys,' cried Mark. 'You can do it, we can do it!'

They did. As they got closer to the valley the herd became ever more restless. Everyone had to work hard to keep them steady, as the last thing David wanted was them stampeding into the narrow confines of the canyon. Bit by bit, though, they managed to push the herd into almost single file and feed them through the tight entrance. Working at the rear of the herd, Caroline and Mark were the last to enter. At once the atmosphere changed. With steep rock faces each side of them, they were protected from the harshness of the sun, and in the distance Caroline could hear water running and soon she saw a steep cascade, tumbling down the almost sheer face of the rock.

'Gotta keep them moving,' said Mark, 'they'll want to drink, but we gotta keep them orderly.'

They pressed on until at last they were past the narrowest of the canyon, and the herd could at last spread out and drink from the creek.

Caroline dismounted and refilled her canteen with the cold, fresh water. David drew alongside and did likewise.

'Dare I say, so far so good?' she said.

'You dare.' He leaned back and took great gulps of water, before refilling his canteen.

'Is it all right if I walk alongside my horse for a while?'

'I'm going to do the same,' he said.

'If this is Mint Creek, where are all the prospectors?' she asked.

He pointed back to the waterfall. 'The creek rises high up on that plateau and runs a few miles before the falls. That's where the prospectors will be, poor devils.'

She walked backwards for a while. 'Now I know you'll think I'm silly, but it would be the most perfect place for a picnic.'

He laughed out loud. 'I sat there once with Grandpa. He'd caught some scrawny old bird and cooked it over his campfire, so I suppose I have had a picnic here. It wasn't very nice. He told me that every waterfall has a secret cave behind it, where magical creatures live.'

'Ah, and you believed him.'

'No, I was twenty-three.'

Now she laughed out loud.

'I didn't meet Grandpa until after Ma died. He'd fallen out with her, for marrying Pa, but they were reconciled at the end.'

'I remember the letter you wrote me, telling me that she'd died, and she'd been buried next to your little brother.' She sighed. 'There was so much that you didn't tell me, though.'

'Didn't think you needed to know,' he said, pulling himself back onto his horse and cantering away.

★   ★   ★

The land began to open up once more, and everyone relaxed as the herd continued amiably alongside the creek. By the time dusk fell Caroline was almost in a trance, suddenly realizing that the herd had stopped and the riders were starting to dismount. Dog tired, but in good spirits they set up their camp for the night.

★   ★   ★

Caroline retrieved a small sewing kit from her bag and settled herself next to a lantern. She had cut some thick fabric from one of the food bags.

David hunched down next to her, frowning.

'I'm getting blisters,' she said showing him her reddened hands. 'I thought if I put an extra layer on the palms of my gloves it would help.'

'You're keeping up better than I thought.' He felt it was only fair to tell her.

She pulled a length of thread, snapped it with her teeth and holding it close to the light threaded it into the eye of the needle.

David pulled off his own gloves, which were much thicker than Caroline's. If they hadn't been his hands would have suffered too, softened as they were by years of office work. He sat silently beside her, as her needle rhythmically pierced the fabric. He jerked slightly at the sound of Tom's voice, realizing he must have drifted off to sleep.

'If you've got the light, miss,' Tom was saying, 'I've got a great rip in my vest, causing me some annoyance.'

'Give it to me, Tom, I'll repair it directly.' Then her needle halted. 'I've stopped smelling the cows, but now I don't even hear them mooing.'

'They are quieter now. It's because they're more settled, ain't they, Young Boss?' said Tom.

But David's head was now lying on his saddle and his breathing was soft and regular.

'Reckon you're on first watch tonight, Boss,' Tom said to Mark.

⋆ ⋆ ⋆

Caroline wasn't sure what actually awoke her. She was lying on the ground, her head was resting on her saddle and someone had put a blanket around her. She certainly couldn't remember falling asleep. She could just make out the embers of the camp-fire and somebody was snoring. In the moonlight she could see that David was still next to her. She reached out and squeezed his arm. He moaned slightly but did not awake. She tugged harder. He coughed.

'What is it?' he whispered. She could hear the concern in his voice.

'I don't know,' she answered. 'Something woke me up, I don't know what.'

'Maybe an insect crawling across your face. Why didn't you sleep in the wagon?'

'I must have fallen asleep here.' She sat up now and shivered slightly, though the night air was not too cold. She could hear the herd moving, there were one or two low moans, then more agitation.

Someone else was awake and creeping over to them.

It was Paulie. 'Something's spooking the herd,' he whispered.

'Cougar? Coyote?' David whispered back, sitting up.

'Could be, I've got my rifle. You know I can shoot the wings off a gnat. Whatever it is, I'll get it.'

'Caro, can you saddle the horses in

this light?' David asked her.

'I'll do my best.'

'Have you seen Pa?' she heard David ask Paulie as they headed off towards the herd.

* * *

It was almost dawn and a thin light began to streak the horizon.

'Over there,' said Paulie, pointing to a rippling in the generally calm livestock.

'I see,' said David. 'Keep to the edge, Paulie, I don't want to get caught up with them if they decide to run.'

'Nor me,' said Paulie walking slowly, keeping his rifle pointed. He span round swiftly at the sound of hoofs, but it was only Caroline leading their horses to them.

'I'll feel better dealing with this from up here,' said David, pulling himself into the saddle, and Paulie, likewise, mounted. David leaned down. 'Can you wake everyone up, quietly?'

The ripple of agitation was moving

into the mass of cows. David and Paulie pushed their way forward.

'Darn it, thought I saw a horse in there,' said David.

'Maybe one got untethered,' said Paulie.

'Let's hope,' said David, suddenly tugging on his reins as several of the cows began to jerk about and one or two tried to make a run for it. 'Keep them tight!' called David, as Paulie galloped around and brought the attempted runaways back into line.

'Help me!' they heard a voice crying softly. 'Help! They're going to stampede.'

'Stay where you are, keep calling,' said David, as he and Paulie steadily parted the animals and headed towards the sound.

The rest of the camp was waking up now. Tom and Flynn were already mounted; Olly was reviving the fire.

The first shaft of light shot across the plain as David eased closer to the plaintive voice.

'Help me, help me, I've lost my horse.'

He could see the man's hat now and gently pushed his way through.

'Oh, thank God, it's you,' said a plainly terrified Sheriff la Bute.

9

La Bute was almost in tears. 'Gotta find my horse,' he sobbed, his breath ragged and panicky.

'Hey, steady, steady,' said David.

'I'll be calm enough when I've found my horse,' he said.

Olly passed him a tin mug and he quickly drank whatever was inside it.

'Reckon I saw a horse in amongst the herd,' said David. 'But it was first thing, the light can play tricks.'

Flynn stood up on his saddle, shielding his eyes from the sun with his hand. 'You're right, Boss,' he said pointing. 'You ride a bony bay?' he asked the sheriff.

'She's a bay, yes. Can you get her? I need my horse, I must have my horse.'

'Steady, feller,' said David. 'We'll get her back for you, seeing the mighty great affection you have for her.' He looked over his shoulder. 'Flynn, Tom, can you cut the sheriff's beloved out for him?'

'Sure thing, Young Boss,' said Tom.

'Well howdy there, Sheriff la Bute,' said Mark riding up. 'Come to escort us to Carlyle?'

La Bute looked affronted. 'I don't care what you do with these filthy animals. I just want my horse. I gotta get back to Clearwater Springs. Dear Lord God Almighty, I hope that kid Paulie's had some sense to cover me with Mr MacPherson.'

Mark smiled, and turned his horse away. 'Get yourselves some food, men,' he said. 'Once we've given the sheriff his horse, we push on.'

'Come to the chuck wagon,' said Caroline to la Bute. 'You got a bad gash to your forehead, were you attacked?'

'No, no, damn fool horse threw me.'

'Come along, I'll wash your wound.'

He pushed her away. 'I ain't bothered about that. I gotta get my horse and back to Clearwater Springs before

Connor MacPherson finds out I'm gone.'

'Ah,' said Caroline softly and went off to get some breakfast. She had just got the spoon to her mouth when the air was rent with the most terrified screaming.

David rushed over to the sheriff and pressed his hand over his mouth. 'That's enough, la Bute, you seem determined to upset my cows.'

The sheriff wriggled and squirmed in his grasp, pointing at one of the hands. It was Caleb.

'No screaming, now,' said David, gently releasing the man.

'W-w-what's he doing here!' he whispered loudly.

'Guess he kind of escaped,' said David.

'I gotta take him back. I need to get back to the jail. It's my jail, I gotta be there. I can't let MacPherson sack me.' He gestured to Caleb. 'Get on your horse, boy, you're coming back with me,' he shouted.

'I sprung Caleb from jail,' said Paulie, sauntering into view, ''cos he should never have been there in the first place. Reckon it's time someone stood up to my dad.'

'Well that ain't gonna be me,' squealed the sheriff. 'I'm taking this boy back. I'll do anything to keep in favour with Mr MacPherson.'

'Oh, it's probably too late for that,' said Paulie carelessly. 'Even Dad will have noticed you, me and Caleb are missing by now.' He laughed, there was a cruel edge to it. 'Lord knows what he thinks we're all up to.'

David felt a soft tap on his shoulder. 'Young Boss,' said Tom, quietly. 'Something you oughta see.'

David walked to the edge of the herd. Flynn was holding la Bute's horse.

'I was just checking her saddle and stuff,' said Tom. 'I wondered if she'd a burr or something to make her throw off her rider. Reckon she was just overloaded.'

Flynn flicked up the flap of the

saddlebag. David looked inside. Gold gleamed up at him, thick ingots of gold. He reached inside, pulled one of them closer to the top, and put on his spectacles so he could read the writing.

'US Treasury,' he said under his breath settling the ingot back into place and putting his glasses back in his pocket.

'I reckon this is Dancing Bird's gold,' said Tom.

'Yeah,' breathed David. 'And la Bute tortured Grandpa to find out where it was, and then cut the old man's throat when he no longer needed him.' He made to set off towards the sheriff, but Tom's strong arms held him back.

'You can't prove that, Young Boss. You've got no more proof on the sheriff than he's got on Caleb.'

'Two saddlebags full of US Treasury gold!'

'Which he could have found. I know, I know, Young Boss, it ain't likely, but rushing in there and giving la Bute a beating ain't going to help.'

'It's gonna help me!' David shrugged off Tom. 'La Bute!' he shouted. 'Would you like to explain to me how come you've got saddlebags full of gold?'

La Bute swivelled round. 'That's sheriff's business, nothing to do with you, breed.'

'It's got everything to do with you killing my grandpa.'

La Bute began to back away. 'Oh no, you ain't going to pin the murder of that scraggy old Indian on me! Did the world a favour anyway,' he added under his breath.

David surged towards him, but la Bute snatched the nearest horse to him, Caleb's, and pulled himself aboard with astonishing agility and galloped head-long away from the herd.

David jumped onto his horse, but Mark blocked his way, reaching down to pull on the reins, using the force of his own, heavier horse to stop David moving. David pulled his gun and aimed it.

'No!' snapped Mark.

'He's Grandpa's murderer.'

'You gotta leave him for now. We've got more important things to do.'

David's breath was ragged. His father was right. He closed his eyes, but all he could see was his grandfather's pathetic body. He felt a soft hand squeeze his leg. He looked down at Caroline.

'David, you can't leave us. This whole drive is your idea.'

'Anyone can punch cows. You picked it up quick enough.'

'Yes, but there's a way to go yet and not one of us here will be able to do the deal with the bank at Carlyle.'

He closed his eyes again and took more deep breaths. She was right, damn her. His pa was a good cattleman, but the business side of it wasn't his strength. He holstered his gun, and heard everyone sigh with relief. He opened his eyes. 'What's with all this hanging around!' he called. 'These steers aren't going to take themselves to Carlyle.'

'Thank you, Caroline,' said Mark softly as he rode alongside her.

'Aw, hell,' moaned Caleb. 'Looks like I'm gonna have to ride the sheriff's old nag.'

'She'll be sprightly enough once I've relieved her of all that gold,' said Tom.

★   ★   ★

David was angry and worked himself to the point of exhaustion. In the end it was Mark who made him stop. 'Maybe you got energy to go all night, but the rest of us ain't.' He called everyone to a halt.

Louisa slid off her horse like butter off a hot knife. She slumped on the ground, unable to move. 'I'd ask you to shoot me, brother,' she said, 'except it would give you too much pleasure.'

Flynn reached down and pulled her upright. 'You sure busted our asses today, Boss,' he said.

'Should've let me go after the sheriff,

then you'd have been able to give yourselves an easy ride, wouldn't you.' He spurred his horse away from them.

'Give him a few minutes, then will you go to him, Caroline?' said Mark.

'If you think it will help, I will,' she said, walking over to Louisa and supporting her from the other side to Flynn. 'Where does it hurt?' she asked.

'I do believe there's a small place behind my left ear that ain't got no pain, otherwise everywhere else. Don't go to him, Caro, he's mean and moody, let him stew.'

'Ah, stew,' said Flynn. 'You know I'm actually looking forward to an Olly special tonight.'

'Don't make me laugh,' gasped Louisa, 'that just hurts too much.'

★ ★ ★

He was standing straight and still, staring at the moon.

'I've brought you some food and

153

coffee,' said Caroline, placing the mug and bowl on a convenient rock.

He showed no sign of having heard her, though he must have done. Louisa was right, she should let him stew.

'I'll go back, then,' she said, turning, but his strong arms grasped her, pulling her so closely to him that she could hardly breathe, then his lips took away what was left of her breath.

⋆ ⋆ ⋆

'Nothing's changed,' he said, smoothing her hair, where his hands had tousled it. 'You're getting on the train at Carlyle.'

'It was unfair of you, then, to kiss me like that.'

'Yep. I just couldn't stop myself. Sorry.'

'Hmm.' They were sitting on the warm earth, she pulled up her knees under her chin. She should have been angry, but couldn't find it in herself to be so. Whether that was due to love or exhaustion she had no idea. 'Your stew's still a bit warm, you must eat, keep up your strength.'

She passed the bowl to him and he obeyed, swiftly finishing it. 'Is it my imagination or is Olly's cooking improving?'

She didn't answer.

He leaned across her and turned up the flame in the hurricane lamp.

'I'd better get back to the others,' she said.

'Why?'

'I don't want to risk you kissing me again, telling me you love me and everything.'

'I won't be kissing you again. I had a moment of weakness, for which I have already apologized.'

She looked at the palms of her hands by the lamplight.

'How are your blisters?' he asked.

The kindness in his voice made her let out a soft sob.

'Oh, Caro — '

She stood up abruptly, with a small gasp of pain as her muscles protested.

'You're not fair, David Merkel, you're not fair at all.'

'No I'm not. I simply wanted to talk to you about Grandpa and the sheriff, the gold and everything.'

'Then ride with me tomorrow and we'll talk. I don't feel I want to be alone with you any more.'

* * *

'Are we in Indian country yet?' Caroline asked David as he brought his horse alongside hers the following morning.

'We have been since we left the canyon.'

'How long till we get to Carlyle, do you think?'

'Two more days I hope. If it takes three we're going to start taking heavy losses. The herd will be really hungry and thirsty crossing the next bit of desert. We've already got a load of stragglers. That's what did for Lou and Flynn yesterday. I've got Pa and Tom on it this morning. Me and Stumpy'll do our bit this afternoon.'

'I could help too. You said I'd learned fast.'

He smiled. 'It might come to that.' They rode in silence for a while. 'About last night,' said David eventually.

'Best not to be mentioned.'

'I wanted to apologize again. I'd got so wound up over the sheriff and Grandpa. Then you were there, and I lost my self-control. It won't happen again, I promise.'

'Oh.'

He showed no indication that he heard the disappointment in her voice.

'You said you wanted to talk to me about the sheriff and Dancing Bird. Why are you so sure la Bute is the murderer?'

'Because he is, I know it!' he said, as if that should be enough.

'You *think* it. La Bute could have come by that gold anywhere, from anyone.'

He raised his eyebrows. 'And how

many times have you tripped over a gold ingot marked US Treasury? I never saw an ingot of any sort before, not even at your pa's bank.'

'Oh, I'm not saying la Bute isn't guilty of something. He was so keen to get back to town and keep in with MacPherson, I'm sure he's got more of those bars hidden away in the jailhouse somewhere.'

'Course he has! Clever you.'

She smiled proudly. 'But that doesn't even begin to prove he was involved in Dancing Bird's death. What if Caleb is guilty? Maybe the sheriff got it out of him, or Caleb was working on making a deal with him.'

'You can't think that,' he said, looking at her askance.

'No I don't. But la Bute's defence lawyer will if he ever stands trial.'

David sighed. 'That ain't going to happen. By the time we get back to Clearwater Springs he'll be long gone.'

'That will depend how many bars are left at Mint Creek. He's got greedy. I reckon he'll try and help himself to a few more. And don't forget, running away with heavy gold ingots won't be easy.'

'All good points. But if that was me I'd take what I could carry and hightail it out of the territory as fast as I could.'

She laughed. 'But you're not greedy or an idiot; la Bute is both of those things.' She kicked Shadow and cantered after half a dozen head who were veering off the trail.

No, thought David, I may not be an idiot, but I sure am a fool.

She came back, breathless and wiping her face with the neckerchief he had given her. 'Heat's really something now, isn't it?'

'I do have another reason for thinking la Bute was involved. Grandpa accused me of following him. He said he could see my spectacles glinting in the dark. I didn't take much notice at the time — Grandpa could come up with some pretty outrageous ideas sometimes.'

'But you only wear your spectacles

for reading; I've never seen you with them on any other time.'

'That's because I only need them for reading. Now, Layton la Bute, I've never seen him *without* his glasses.'

She let out a long breath. 'I still don't think that'll stand up in court. Even if la Bute was following him, it doesn't mean he killed your grandpa.'

'I know, Caro. Yesterday I was convinced he'd done it. I'm still sure, but I know I can't prove it. The worrying thing is I nearly killed a man because I had a feeling. What sort of a savage does that make me?'

'You *nearly* killed a man, David. Nearly is the important word. That's what stops you being a savage.' She pointed to another little group of cows who'd decided to go their own way. 'Your turn,' she said with a smile.

David wheeled his horse round, grim-faced. He couldn't stop thinking about their kiss. He could have that, and more, any time he wanted, yet he was going to do his darndest to make sure that girl got on the train back East. He wasn't an idiot, he wasn't a savage, but a damn, damn fool, that was a charge of which he was completely guilty.

10

Early the next morning a small group of Apache appeared as if from nowhere. Caroline felt some tension in the hands, but David was relaxed enough.

'You drive a tight herd, brother,' said one to David.

'We're doing all right, thanks to you letting us trail over your land,' said David. 'Cut out a few head if you can use them.'

'Many thanks for that.' The Indian shot a glance at Caroline, then returned his attention to David and gave him a conspiratorial smile. 'I wish you well, brother.'

★   ★   ★

By the evening the herd had been steered away from the creek and were headed out into the desert again. This

162

time the moon was brighter and they kept going for most of the night. It was nearly midday the next day when Stumpy pointed to the horizon.

'Is that dust or smoke?' he called.

David held up his hand and everyone pulled up their horses. He stood up in his stirrups and squinted. 'I can't tell.'

Flynn did his favourite party piece of standing on his saddle and put the spy glass to his eye. 'It's smoke. It's a town. It's Carlyle!' he shouted. 'We done it, Young Boss! We done it.' He slipped back into the saddle, cantered over to David and slapped him on the back. 'Young Boss, I take it all back. I said it could never be done. Can you drive cattle!'

David allowed himself a stiff smile. 'It's nearly done,' he said. 'Who's got the fastest horse?'

'That would be Miss Fisher,' said Caleb.

David dismounted and went over to her. 'Get down,' he said. 'We need to

163

send someone ahead of us.'

'I'm happy to do that.'

'Well I ain't happy to let you.' He reached up, grabbed her around the waist and pulled her off. 'Change saddles, Flynn,' he said to the hand, 'and get to Carlyle as fast as you can. Tell them we'll be there before nightfall. You find the cattle merchant and tell him how many head we're bringing. Anyone you can get to help I'll stand them a drink. Once the herd smells water they'll be coming in a bit boisterous, so it'll be a struggle to keep it orderly.'

Flynn was smiling broadly as he threw his saddle over Shadow's back. 'I'll be darned! I never thought we'd do it. Thought we'd have nothing left but skeletons. You're one top man, Young Boss, one top cattle driver.' He jumped onto Shadow and thundered off.

Caroline was not happy. 'I could easily have done that,' she protested.

David snorted. 'If you really thought I'd let you ride alone through the desert

164

and into a strange town, you don't know me at all. Now saddle up Flynn's horse and get back to work.'

★   ★   ★

The last push was hard. As David predicted the herd knew something was happening, and tired, hungry and thirsty as they were, they became more skittish. About an hour outside Carlyle, Flynn returned with a sizable number of volunteers. 'We're famous!' he cried. 'No one believes we've had the grit to bring our cows across Indian country and the desert.'

★   ★   ★

Getting the restive herd into the cattle pens was achieved in a somewhat messy way, but with no injuries to any of the hands, despite the inconvenience of the sizable crowd that had come to meet them.

'I never expected this, son,' said

Mark, as they finally closed the gate on the last steer.

A man carrying a large camera on a tripod came up to them. 'I believe you're both Mr Merkel, father and son. I'd be grateful if you'd pose for a shot, for posterity and for the *Carlyle Informer*.'

Dazed by tiredness and this unexpected reception, David and Mark slid from their horses, and by the time the camera had been set up were joined by Louisa and Flynn, who seemed more than happy to pose for posterity and the local press.

The reporter now took his pencil and notebook from his pocket. 'Right then, gentlemen and ladies, I'll need your names.'

As Louisa happily recited everyone's names, David and Mark were approached by a middle-aged man of unremarkable features, wearing a smart dark suit with a bootlace tie and a broad, cream-coloured Stetson.

He held out his hand. 'Nehemiah

Rice, cattle merchant,' he introduced himself. 'And are you an answer to prayer.'

'Are we?' said David, shaking his hand.

'Indeedy you are. There's a train due at the end of the week. It was breaking my heart that I was going to have to send it back empty.'

'You offer us the right price, you have your train load,' said David.

'We'll deal,' said Rice, pointing towards the low hut that, presumably, was his office.

Inside was far more comfortable than the outside would suggest. They walked through a small anteroom. Rice asked the clerk sitting there to bring in whiskey, and ushered David and Mark into his office. They settled themselves into two comfortable chairs. Rice took his seat and raised his glass.

'Audacious, that's what everyone is saying, audacious.'

They all took a sip and put their glasses back on the desk.

'Let's negotiate, shall we?' said David.

★ ★ ★

Caroline stood a little away from the crowd as Louisa and Flynn, who had now been joined by the rest of the hands, eagerly told the journalist the story of their epic journey. A man sidled up to her. She turned to face him. The badge on his chest read 'US Marshal'.

'Sorry to interrupt,' he said with a polite nod of his head, 'but I couldn't help overhearing that you gave your name as Caroline Fisher.'

'That's right,' she said.

The marshal continued. 'I had a man come into my office yesterday, asking me a deal of questions about Clearwater Springs and the ranches around there. His name was Hunter F. Dutton.'

She looked bemused. 'I've never heard that name before.'

'Well, he reckoned he was an attorney at law, under the instruction of a Miss Caroline Fisher of Vermont.'

The lawyer! She had completely forgotten about that. 'I don't know him, Marshal, but I think he must be the attorney hired by my father, on my behalf, to give a friend of ours some advice.'

'That'll be some hefty advice then, miss. The man says he comes from New York City.'

'Has he already left for Clearwater Springs?'

'No ma'am, he's holed up at the Majestic Hotel waiting for the next stage.'

'Then I shall seek him out. Thank you for letting me know, Marshal.'

*   *   *

Rice, Mark and David shook hands.

'I'll call that a done deal,' said Rice with satisfaction, 'just bear with me a moment.' He went briefly into the anteroom, then came back and refilled their glasses.

Rice rolled his glass between his fingers. 'I like your plans. I like the way you think about business. I always use Smith's Bank in Carlyle, I've never had a reason to cuss them. I'd be happy to recommend them.'

'Whichever bank we use, I've gotta get something sorted out tomorrow,' said David.

Rice raised his glass again. 'I'm going to sleep on it, but I'm thinking I might do some investing in you. Yes, I think I might. And to mark your achievement I've booked you all into the Majestic Hotel for the night, my treat.'

'Darn,' said David. 'If I'd known you'd got money to burn I'd have stuck out for five cents a head more.'

Rice chuckled and shook his head. 'Two at most. You didn't make too bad a bargain. Your cattle drive was amazing, but your herd are a scrawny bunch, and I don't think that's all to do with the desert, either.'

'We did all right, son,' said Mark to David, before turning to the cattle merchant. 'I'll be honest, we'd hit a bad patch, but this is the start of better days. Many, many thanks to you, Mr Rice.'

'Come and see me first thing tomorrow morning,' said the merchant.

★ ★ ★

Caroline was about to make her way into town when she heard a cheer go up from the hands as Mark and David left the cattle merchant's office. She turned around and as David came out he punched the air. She knew he'd done the deal.

As for David he was happy enough to call the hands around him, pay them at last and tell them about their rooms at the hotel.

'The Majestic Hotel,' said Caroline as he walked towards her. 'I was just setting off there.'

'I believe there's a train due in a couple of days,' said David. 'I'll go to the station and find out.'

'No, please come to the hotel with me first,' she said and told him about Hunter F. Dutton.

'Caleb's attorney's here, Pa,' said David to his father.

'I don't know where Caleb's gone,' said Mark.

'Never mind,' said Caroline. 'I intend to introduce myself to Mr Dutton right away.'

★   ★   ★

The waiter indicated a large man, dominating a round table in the corner of the dining room. As they walked towards him they could see he was engaged in something of a battle with the steak the size of a saddle. He was winning.

'Sorry to disturb you, Mr Dutton,' said Caroline, 'but I am Caroline Fisher of Waverley, Vermont. I believe my father has engaged your services.'

Hunter looked up, swiftly rose to his feet and offered his hand. 'Why, hello,

172

Miss Fisher,' he said, not making any effort to hide his admiration. Then he looked over her shoulder and raised an eyebrow.

'Let me introduce you to my associates, Mr Mark and Mr David Merkel,' she said.

Smiling broadly Hunter offered his surprisingly small hand, considering his bulk, to both of the men. 'Ah, Mr David Merkel is your fiancé, I believe, Miss Fisher.'

'No, I'm not her fiancé,' said David, 'but it's good to make your acquaintance, sir.'

Caroline smiled inwardly as he was showing the sort of respect he always showed her father, and which he rarely seemed to display to anyone in the West.

'Please carry on with your meal, don't let your steak get cold,' said Caroline.

'Do I look like a man who lets his steak get cold?' said Hunter, settling himself into his seat. 'Join me, I reckon you could all do with a drink.' He waved his hand in the direction of the waiter.

'Three beers,' said Mark when the waiter joined them. 'What would you like, Mr Dutton?'

The lawyer indicated a bottle of red wine in front of him. 'I'm happy enough with my friend here at the moment.'

The waiter hesitated slightly, then leaned towards David. 'I'm sorry, boy,' he said softly. 'It ain't your fault, I don't suppose you can read or write, but there's a notice on the door clearly states 'No Indians'.'

'Are you accusing my son of being an Indian, simply because he's picked up a bit of trail dust?' said Mark.

Caroline saw the corners of Hunter's mouth twitch, as he continued with his heroic chewing.

'This boy is your son, sir?' said the waiter.

'This man is, yes. Folks say we're like two peas in a pod. Don't tell me you can't see the likeness?'

The waiter's mouth twisted uncomfortably. 'Well, of course I can, sir. But it's not me, it's the manager,' he finished lamely. Then he looked at Caroline. 'And, miss, I think the manager might be a little worried about your attire.'

'He's no need to be, it's totally comfortable,' she replied sweetly.

Hunter was chuckling openly, now. 'Just get them their beers, good man,' he said with a dismissive flick of the wrist.

'So, Miss Fisher,' said Hunter. 'I have only the briefest of briefs, concerning a man by the name of Caleb, who, you say, is wrongly charged with murder.'

'Arrested and imprisoned on suspicion of murder,' said Caroline, 'and on the slenderest of evidence.'

'Right, give me the full details.'

'There is one detail I should perhaps tell you first,' said Caroline.

Hunter raised an eyebrow.

'Caleb isn't exactly in jail at the moment.'

The three of them proceeded to tell Hunter the full story. He had finished his steak by the time they fell silent.

'My, my,' he said, leaning back in the chair that seemed far too delicate to support his bulk. 'Thank you for that. Now, I've been making some inquiries while waiting for the stage. The marshal here seems a decent enough man, and he's of the opinion the sheriff of Clearwater Springs is no legal sheriff at all, simply being in the employ of a man named MacPherson, who allows him to use that title.'

'I knew it!' exclaimed David, slapping his thigh, setting off a puff of dust. 'La Bute is a villain if I ever saw one.' He went on to outline his theories concerning la Bute's involvement with his grandfather's death.

Hunter poured the last of his wine into his glass, and rubbed his hand across his forehead. 'Looks like I might have a two-steak case on my hands,' he said.

'You might have two cases if you agree to prosecute la Bute,' said David.

Hunter held up his hand. 'Steady on, young fellow. Your theories concerning the implication of guilt, due to the wearing of spectacles, don't impress me much. To get a conviction you've got to prove beyond reasonable doubt the accused is guilty. From what you've told me, I've got genuine reasonable doubts that either of these men is a murderer, though I agree, the so-called sheriff's behaviour is suspicious. I'd dearly like to know more about that gold, too.' He sighed, yawned, then held his hands in front of him and clicked his fingers. 'I've got a lot of thinking to do, and I need to speak to Caleb, who is my client, after all. Tonight is not the night for that. You've all completed this magnificent cattle drive that everyone's talking about, and you need to have a rest, and, um, freshen up a little, if you don't mind me saying so.'

'We'll leave you in peace for now then, Mr Dutton,' said Caroline, looking up as Louisa swept into the room.

'My daughter — ' began Mark.

'Isn't this a marvellous place!' she exclaimed breathlessly, spinning round. 'Caro, I've ordered a bath, come and share the water with me.'

Caroline didn't need to be asked twice. 'Tomorrow then,' she said as Louisa grabbed her hand and pulled her from the room.

Hunter's eyes, which until then had been narrow and almost reptilian, became round as buttons, as he watched the two women with undisguised appreciation. Then he looked to his remaining companions. 'Sorry, gentlemen,' he said. 'I know one's your daughter, and the other your fiancée, but a man's a man.'

'Miss Fisher ain't my fiancée,' said David, firmly.

Hunter's eyes narrowed again. 'Then any business I have with your family will be with your father, because I won't take on a fool as a client.'

★ ★ ★

Marshal Cox let out a long breath and stared at the ingots David had placed on his desk. Then he took in another deep one, and released that slowly. 'My word,' he said at length.

'Umm,' said David. 'Do you have any thoughts?'

'Not really, save that wherever the man Layton la Bute found this gold, it sure as hell wasn't the US Treasury.'

'No, even he wasn't claiming that. There's every indication it was hidden somewhere at Mint Creek. We have the feeling la Bute may have more concealed in the jail at Clearwater Springs, and we've no way of knowing if there's any more at the Creek.'

'Nooo,' said Cox, sighing heavily again. 'Right, young man, I'm going to write you a receipt for this and lock it in my safe. Then I'm going to see Judge

Frixell and find out what he thinks.'

'Very well,' said David. He had more than enough to think about for the time being and was glad to have relinquished the gold.

11

'Pleased to meet you, Caleb,' boomed Hunter, pumping his client's hand. 'Right then. Let me introduce myself, I am Hunter Frederick Dutton, attorney at law.' He handed Caleb one of his business cards. 'I can assure you my qualifications are genuine, I studied law at Harvard, and gained a first class degree. I have been instructed by Horace Fisher of Waverley in Vermont and he has given me permission to talk directly about your case to his daughter, Caroline Fisher, here present. If that's all right with you, Caleb.'

Caleb nodded.

'We'll start with a few formalities. What's your full name, Caleb?'

Caleb looked blank. 'Always known as Caleb, sir.' He turned to Caroline. 'It's mighty good of your pa to do this for me, miss. Don't know how I'll ever repay him.'

'No, that's all sorted,' she said kindly. 'You have a surname, don't you?'

Caleb shrugged. 'My parents were owned by a man named Stone. Reckon that'll make me Caleb Stone. Yes, sir, that can be my full name if you like.'

'I don't particularly like,' said Hunter, writing it down, 'but it will have to do for the moment. Now, Mr Stone, would you tell me exactly what happened on the day you were arrested?'

★ ★ ★

Nehemiah Rice was a sharp, shrewd businessman who could strike a hard bargain, but he was also a romantic, and something about the plucky young half-breed and his motley group of helpers, crossing the desert and trying to save their ranch, appealed to that softer side. Using his extensive contacts, by the time David came to see

182

him that morning, he already had some ideas where some young breeding animals could be sourced, and even accompanied David to the bank. This, David was quick to acknowledge, made the task of setting up a loan far easier than he had feared. With Mr Rice as both an investor (if modest) and supporter, the manager of the bank was, David suspected, rather more amenable than he would have been if he had visited him alone. With the business of the day completed much sooner than he expected, David had plenty of time to go to the station and take notes of the times of the trains and the connections Caroline would have to make to return to Vermont.

★　★　★

Hunter had written copious notes. 'I think that will do for now,' he said closing his notebook. 'I shall keep to my plan and journey to Clearwater Springs by the next stage.'

'Are the problems with the stage sorted out, then?' asked Mark.

Hunter said he didn't know there had been any.

Mark shot Caroline a sideways look.

'I crossed my fingers when I said it,' she said with a smile.

'Miss Fisher, will you be accompanying me?' asked Hunter.

Mark leaned towards her. 'Remember you're my guest and can stay as long as you like. And as soon as we've got a new herd I shall need all my experienced cowmen.'

'David is determined that I return to Vermont,' she said.

'That won't do at all,' said Hunter. 'Now, Mr Merkel, Miss Fisher, I'll say good day to you. I need to spend a short while alone with my client now.'

* * *

David saw Caroline coming out of the hotel. She waved at him, and he quickly

184

caught up with her. She explained she had left Caleb with Hunter.

'What does he think?' asked David.

'He didn't say, but looking at his face I think he thinks that if it comes to trial it could go against Caleb. The jailbreak hasn't helped.'

'Let's just hope it doesn't come to trial, then. If it does I shall make sure Paulie testifies for him.' He handed her a piece of paper. 'The next train is Friday. That's a list of your connections.'

'Thank you,' she said. 'I've been offered a job, though.'

'Oh?'

'Yes, your pa's hired me as a hand when you get your new herd.'

'He had no right to do that. You're going home, Caroline.'

'Your pa can hire who he likes, and it's not for you to say what I do or don't do. You don't own me.' She paused and a small smile twisted the corners of her lips. 'Strange, isn't it, if you'd stuck to your original plan and married me, you would own me. So, what's happening?'

'Mr Rice knows of a herd for sale that might be suitable, though I don't know if we're up for another drive back the way we came. The loan is sorted out already.'

'What, you've got the money!' She reached forward and hugged him; he didn't have time to avoid her. 'You must tell your father immediately. Why didn't you say anything?'

'I just did. Anyway I'm preoccupied with getting you out of this town.'

She turned away from him and headed back to the hotel. 'If you don't want to tell Mark, I shall.'

*　*　*

By the afternoon Mr Rice had some more good news for David concerning some very reasonably priced heifers and a couple of bulls he could purchase, and he would not have to travel too far out of his way to collect them. Rice's romantic side fully in control now, he paid for another night at the Majestic and promised to join everyone at the hotel that evening for a meal. David's grave expression confused him. 'Thought you'd be pleased, David,' he said, as he himself was beaming from ear to ear.

'Yes, I am, and very conscious of your help and grateful for it, Mr Rice. I just think I've got a lot on my mind at the moment, that's all. The hands are all up for the drive back, but I just keep thinking, can we do it again, or did we just get lucky?'

Rice slapped him on the shoulder. 'You're dog-tired. I keep forgetting what a journey you had to get here. You get yourself some shut-eye and I'll see you this evening. I'm sure looking forward to meeting the rest of your team, especially those lovely ladies. I believe one's your sister — who's the other?'

'Just someone I know, um, a sort of friend.'

Rice chortled. 'You're a lucky man

then, young David. All my friends look like me.'

★ ★ ★

Back at the hotel, David had a message to see Mr Dutton in his room.

The big man yawned enormously as he opened the door. 'Doesn't this heat send you to sleep in the afternoon?' he asked as he motioned David inside. 'I suppose you're used to it. Good news about the ranch. Seems like your plan is coming together at last.' He yawned again. 'I find a little nip of brandy perks me up no end at this time of day.' He filled two glasses and handed one to David. 'I understand you expect Miss Fisher to be on the eastbound train on Friday.'

David took a tiny polite sip and put the glass back on the table. 'Yes, that's right.'

'I'm afraid I can't allow that to happen,' said Hunter, draining his glass and immediately refilling it.

'She's going, I've made up my mind.'

Hunter's eyes narrowed and his expression lost any hint of the bonhomie it had previously shown. 'It's not up to you, is it?'

'And it's none of your business, either.' David turned towards the door.

'It is. Don't leave, hear me out. I am engaged by Caroline's father. She is his representative. As long as he wants me to represent Caleb, and believe me, if there's a trial Caleb's going to need me, then I need to have Miss Fisher with me. Now, you can either let her travel back with you, or she can return to Clearwater Springs with me on the stage. If you don't want her at the ranch, we'll arrange our own accommodation.'

David felt anger rising inside him. He hated being dictated to. 'I don't think that's strictly true. As long as Horace Fisher pays the bill Caleb is represented. I can't see any need for Caroline to stay in Arizona at all. I don't know what game you're playing,

Mr Dutton, but you gotta believe me, it's best for everyone, especially Caroline, if she's on that train on Friday.'

'Oh, don't think I don't understand your reasons, which are crystal clear. You imagine you're saving Caroline from all the insults, abuse and prejudice you think she'll have to endure if she marries you.'

'That's exactly what I know she'll have to endure. At least you understand I do have her best interests in mind.'

Hunter grunted. 'I'm not sure about that. You'll break her heart; I don't think that's in her best interests. If she can't have you what will happen to her? She might settle for someone for whom she has nothing more than vague affection. Why make her do that when you will be magnificent together? Go to her, be with her, love her, and challenge the world together. Nobody has a straight run through life. I'm not saying it will be easy for either of you, but how can things change when good people don't bother to fight?'

David had had enough. He grabbed Hunter's braces, shook him and then threw him backwards. The big man stumbled, and only stopped falling to the floor by grabbing the bed post.

David was snarling, his breath panting harshly. 'You can stop your patronizing sermons, white man, because you've got no idea what it's like to be me. Being married to a half-breed isn't just not having a straight run at life; it would mean being despised. When your client, Mr Horace Fisher of Waverley, Vermont found out my ma was a squaw it changed everything, and Mr Fisher, I know, is a good man. He denounced me, in front of everyone. My colleagues, his family, everyone I had known and respected. But in minutes they lost all respect for me. He'd encouraged me to court Caroline, but when he knew I was a breed the very thought of me being anywhere near her made his flesh crawl. Yes, since then, he's thought about it, taken some guidance from the Good Book, and repented. I'm happy to forgive. But I can't forget, Mr Dutton, because I was there. I was shamed and vilified, and all because I'm not white. Now Mr Fisher is a good man, how do you think Caroline will fare against the wicked?'

Hunter grunted loudly as he pulled himself upright, puffing heavily. 'Oh yes, it's all about you, isn't it, boy? Well I'm going to do something I don't usually do. I'm going to give some advice, free of charge. You've got a load of pride to shed, and a deal of climbing down from that high horse you're mounted on before you're worthy of Caroline Fisher, and that's got nothing to do with you being a breed. And think on this, why did you let yourself be passed off as a white man for so long? I'd hate to think you're ashamed of what you are, because you shouldn't be. But you got found out, didn't you, boy, and that's what really hurt.'

David was done talking. His fists

lashed out and pummelled into Hunter, and as he was such a large target he hit him time and time again, while the attorney flailed his arms and tried to push him off. Eventually David pulled back, gasping. 'Don't ever call me 'boy' again,' he said.

Hunter laughed and wiped his mouth, looking bemused, as if he couldn't work out why his handkerchief was stained with blood.

'You think this is funny?' said David.

Hunter sat on the side of his bed, still dabbing his mouth and chuckling. 'You didn't hit me because I called you 'boy',' he said.

David felt confused. He hadn't liked the things that Hunter said. He pointed his finger. 'You just get Caleb off this charge, eh, Dutton, or I'll give you a beating that splits a damn sight more than your lip.'

Hunter was really laughing now.

Confused, upset and somehow, though he didn't know why, ashamed, David stormed out of the room.

'You look like a man in a hurry,' called Marshall Cox, peeping out from the jailhouse door, as David marched, sightless with anger, past him. 'You got a minute for me, Mr Merkel? I think you'll find what I've got to say mighty interesting.'

David sighed, swallowed hard and silently counted to ten before turning. 'Go on then, Marshal, interest me.'

The law man beckoned him inside. For some reason he kept a stove burning in his office, which made it unbearably hot. He poured David a coffee from the pot that stood on the stove. David took a few tentative sips — it wasn't for the fainthearted.

'I've discovered quite a bit,' said Cox, settling into his chair and hoisting his legs onto the desk. 'Three strongboxes of US Treasury ingots were stolen from an armoured train carriage some fifteen years ago, so I reckon we can assume that's where your gold is from.'

David sat up and dared another mouthful of coffee. 'You're right, I'm interested, go on.'

Cox removed his legs from the desk and leaned towards David. 'Three men got arrested for the crime, but not all of the gold was recovered. Two of the villains, Abel Chancellor and Sammy Wood, got sent to Yuma. They're due out next spring. The third member of the gang — '

'Layton la Bute,' interjected David.

Cox nodded. 'The same. He turned prosecution witness, and got sentenced on a lesser charge.'

'Fifteen years for stealing gold bars; I've known men hang for less,' said David.

'Dead men can't lead Treasury agents to the stolen ingots, can they?' said Cox with a wry smile.

'Have you notified the Treasury?' asked David.

'Didn't think it was up to me, I'll leave that to Judge Frixell, if he thinks we should.'

David's mind whizzed as he finished his coffee. 'I'm thinking Chancellor and Wood never told la Bute where they hid the gold.'

'Reckon so. I imagine he knew it was in the area of Clearwater Springs, otherwise it's too much of a coincidence that he pitched up there.'

'Yes it would be,' said David.

'Your grandfather found the gold, but he made the mistake of talking about it.'

David breathed out a long sigh.

Cox continued. 'Your theory makes a lot of sense now. It may well be that it was la Bute that beat the information out of the poor old man, and then killed him.'

'One thing is for sure,' said David, grim-faced, 'la Bute must realize that once his partners are released and find out what he's done, he's got a life expectancy that makes a Mayfly look like Methuselah.'

'Beautifully put,' said Cox. 'If the man's not a complete fool he'll try to get himself and as much of the gold as he can to Mexico.'

'He must have ingots hidden in Clearwater. He was desperate to get back and to keep his job as sheriff.'

'My view is he'll hightail it down south just as soon as he can. He may already be on his way as I speak, but I've sent Marshal Sykes up to Clearwater Springs to see what he can find. He's one of my best men. I've spoken to Judge Frixell. He's mighty interested, but, though he agrees I've got enough evidence for questioning, he ain't so sure there's enough proof to get a conviction for murder. Maybe you'd like to consult your fancy-jack lawyer on that.'

David stood up. 'I appreciate all your work, Marshal.'

'I'll let you know if I hear anything else.'

'We're picking up a new herd tomorrow,' said David. 'So I reckon this might be the last time we speak.' He held out his hand and Cox gripped it firmly.

'Good luck with that, then, young feller. You've put in a deal of hard work and no little imagination into saving your pa's ranch. I wish you well.'

★ ★ ★

Despite the fact that Marshal Cox was doing his best to find the killer of Dancing Bird, David couldn't raise his mood, and he sat stony-faced during the evening meal. Nobody seemed to notice, though. Everyone else was in high spirits, and, as Nehemiah and Hunter were both enthusiastic tellers of diverting anecdotes, the evening was enjoyable.

As they prepared to retire to their rooms Mark made sure he had a moment alone with Hunter.

'So, you say you got those bruises falling over,' he said.

Hunter felt his cheeks. 'Fell right on the bed post, clumsy of me.'

'Now you don't strike me as a clumsy man, sir, and I just happen to notice my son's knuckles are raw, and I know he's a bit too hasty with his fists.'

Hunter smiled blandly. 'I'll just keep to my bed post story.'

Mark rubbed his chin. 'Well, I'll not call a distinguished attorney a liar, but I doubt that answer would stand up under cross-examination. However, if you've had a fight with my son and you wish to keep it private, I'll not interfere. I do hope it doesn't affect us, because I have a favour to ask you.'

'If, and this is purely hypothetical, if I had a disagreement with your son, then it would certainly not affect in any way the regard I have for you. And, hypothetically again, if I am at odds with your son, it's because I think he's a grand lad, and I'd hate to see him ruined by bitterness and loneliness brought on by his own stubbornness.'

'Ah,' said Mark, wondering what fancy language Hunter used in court, if this was how he spoke on a hotel landing. 'But hypo this and that aside, will you do me a great favour?'

'Name it, my friend.'

Mark handed him a large envelope. 'These are the documents relating to the loan and the bank transfer. You'll get to Clearwater before we do. Can you make sure this gets to the bank manager there? I think there's less likely to be any argument if it comes from an illustrious person like yourself.'

Hunter took the package. 'Consider it done. Have you told David you're using me as messenger?'

'Yes, and whatever your hypo-whatever argument might be, he could see the good sense of it.'

Hunter tapped the envelope. 'I shall guard this with my very life. Now, Mark, why not come back to my room and have a few shots of brandy with me.'

Mark shook his head. 'That's a tempting offer, but we're off at daybreak tomorrow, and I have prom-ised my children I'll stay off big liquor drinking for a while.'

'Then I'll bid you goodnight, and we'll next meet in Clearwater Springs.'

12

Nehemiah Rice accompanied the River Bow team to the ranch he recommended. The heifers were of a smaller breed than Mark was used to, but as they looked perky and well, he agreed to the purchase. Having said fond and thankful farewells to the cattle merchant, they began the drive back.

Now that they were familiar with the territory and their own routines they made excellent progress for the first day and night and they reached the creek before dawn. They settled into their camp for what was left of the night, sitting in groups around the camp-fire, talking softly.

'I was Marcus van der Merkel then,' David heard his father tell Caroline. 'Fourteen years old and working at the docks in Rotterdam — that's in Holland. All I heard everyone talk of was 'in America this' and 'in America, that'.'

'So you decided to stow away?' she asked.

'Well I didn't have a grand plan, I just walked on board and didn't get off.'

David smiled. It was one of his father's favourite stories. It was good to hear him tell it again.

Olly, Stumpy and Caleb were playing cards. Tom was reading the Bible with his eyes closed and Louisa and Flynn were joshing and giggling together in their usual way.

David waved Paulie over. 'Shall we ride round the herd? They seem quiet enough, but I like to check.'

*　*　*

'I'm just hoping there'll be no trouble with the stage and Hunter will get there in time to do the business,' said Mark as they set off the next morning.

'He'll do fine,' said David. 'Hunter's

sure to get to Clearwater before the end of the month, we probably won't. He's got all the paperwork and he's a difficult man to argue with.'

'Seems you managed, son,' said Mark. 'Can't for the life of me think why, I reckon him a fine fellow.'

'He reckons himself a fine fellow, he don't need any help on that score. If you go round offering advice where it's not needed, you gotta take the consequences.'

Mark laughed. 'Advice you didn't want to hear, more like,' he said, spurring his horse off towards the head of the herd.

Caroline nudged Shadow closer to him. 'I'm sure whatever Hunter said, he meant well.'

David snorted. 'Why is it everyone thinks they gotta give me the benefit of their opinions? Why can't they just leave me to sort things out for myself?'

They jumped as rifle fire cracked above them, the herd instantly becoming restless.

'Up on the bluff over there.' Paulie pointed to a spiky outcrop of rocks.

There was another sally of gunfire, into the cattle. A couple of them were hit and jumped and staggered. Whoever it was attacking them, it was clear their aim was to stampede the herd.

'Damn it!' cried David, galloping closer to the ever more distressed cows. 'Keep them together!'

The final cracks of gunfire were enough to do the trick, and some of the cattle began to speed up, barging into their neighbours, which produced more pressure, and the inevitable rush. David and all the hands galloped after the frightened animals. He managed a swift glance back, though, and saw his father indicating to Caroline to stay behind, and for once she seemed to have taken the advice. With one less thing to worry about, he put himself wholeheartedly into the most urgent task. He was soon up at the head of the herd. Caleb and Tom were already there, trying to steer the leading animals across and stop their mad dash. Already they had lost a few who had fallen, some would doubtless have to be shot, but the tactic was working, and the pace was slowing. David pushed his game pinto even faster. The horse was enjoying the chase, ears pricked well forward. Then, suddenly it stumbled, its front hoof falling into a slight hollow, and David heard the ominous crack, which meant its leg was broken. Such was the speed they were travelling that David was rocketed over the horse's outstretched neck, and dashed into the hot earth. For a moment he could do nothing, as there was no breath in his body. He could feel the stampede vibrating through the earth towards him. He had to move. A rush of air painfully filled his lungs and he managed to stagger to his feet. A wall of cattle was sweeping relentlessly towards him. He stood no chance of outrunning them. He yelled at the top of his voice and waved his arms, but they did not slow. Then he heard the thunder of hoofs behind him and someone was shouting. He swung around. Paulie was belting towards him.

'Catch hold!' he was screaming, 'Catch hold!' He brought his mount right up to David, stopping to a juddering halt, and he leant down and helped David, who was swinging off the pommel, make the most undignified ascent onto a horse. Not that style mattered and with David only half aboard Paulie swung around and dug in his spurs. Confused, Paulie's horse stamped and snorted, then, as David felt the hot breath of the cattle on his body, it sprang into life and galloped its untidy riders out of danger.

★   ★   ★

Before long the herd lost its energy, and a more sensible pace was being restored. Paulie returned to the rear of the herd, where Olly kept the spare horses. David was grateful to slip onto the ground. He held up his hand to Paulie. 'Reckon I owe you one, friend,' he said.

'You don't,' said Paulie.

Mark cantered up, pulling off his hat and wiped his dust-smeared face. 'What happened?'

'Lost my pinto,' said David, tightening the girth on one of the spare horses. 'Nearly lost me too, but thanks to Paulie that didn't happen.' He jumped aboard. 'Are we going to stop them or keep them moving, Pa?'

'Let's slow them down a bit more, they've already lost the will to run. I don't think we're too far off course, either,' said Mark replacing his hat and pulling his neckerchief over his nose. 'Do you reckon the Apache ain't too keen on us making a return journey?'

David frowned and shook his head. 'I'm sure they'd show their faces.'

'I can think of one coward who'd hide his face. I think it's my dad up there,' said Paulie pointing to the bluff.

'Could be,' said Mark. 'Seems like he's not even pretending to give us to the end of the month to pay any more. Looks like it's got personal.'

'Where's Caroline?' said David looking anxiously around.

'She's all right, son,' said Mark. 'She's got the sense to know when she'll be a hindrance, not a help. She stayed out of trouble when we had the stampede, but she's off with Caleb now, bringing in stragglers, which she's very good at. Come on then, you two, let's have a bit of work from you! Though I reckon I owe you, Paulie.'

'No one owes me anything,' said Paulie.

'Hold on a minute!' shouted Olly, who'd been standing on the tailboard of the wagon, scanning the horizon with his telescope.

'What've you seen?' asked David.

'Damn it, it's gone, but for one little moment I thought I saw a solitary rider at the crest of those rocks.'

'Just one man, you sure?' said Mark,

holding his hand above his eyes.

'Darndest thing though, Boss,' continued Olly. 'It looked to me like Caleb's horse, and we know who stole that, don't we?'

'La Bute,' breathed David. 'Damn the man. Looks like he's still in with MacPherson.'

★ ★ ★

The hands were all gathering to share their experiences. Caroline was pleased she'd had no idea how close to death David had been. She felt sick to her stomach, much worse than when the herd had stampeded.

'Did your life flash before you?' she asked.

'No, it didn't,' he said with a slight smile. 'I just thought 'this is going to hurt'.'

'Urgh,' she shivered, 'I can't bear to think of that.'

'We've had to shoot ten, Young Boss,' said Flynn, 'and reckon another seven more at least were trampled to death.'

'Damn,' said David. 'We were doing so well. And we've gotta presume MacPherson's men are still up in those rocks. We'd best keep as far away from them as possible.'

'I agree,' said Mark. 'We've got to be on our guard, he's sure to try something else.'

'Yup,' said Flynn. He turned to Caroline. 'Glad you didn't see what happened to the Young Boss, miss. You were almost a widow before you're a wife. And after what he did, you gotta have Paulie as your best man.' Seeing the expression on David's face, he tipped his hat to Caroline and rode off.

'Why doesn't anyone believe I'm not going to marry you?' David snarled to her under his breath.

'I don't know,' she replied. 'You've made it very clear to me.'

* * *

210

Everyone was relieved when nightfall came and they could rest their aching bodies.

'I've gotta have a whiskey tonight, son,' said Mark to David, 'or these old bones of mine will keep me up all night.'

'You ain't that old. Have your whiskey, but keep alert. We could still be under attack at any time.' He paused. 'I was thinking of going up into those rocks to see if MacPherson's still got any men up there. I want to know what I'm up against.'

Mark groaned. 'I ain't happy with that, son. If MacPherson and his men are hiding up there then you're putting yourself in danger. If there's no one there, it don't mean there won't be someone attacking us tomorrow. I nearly lost you today, son, and I didn't like the feeling. Best thing is to pray for a good day's drive tomorrow.'

David said nothing, but he didn't agree. So far MacPherson had been a vicious and tenacious enemy. There was nothing to suggest he would back off now.

Paulie was thinking along similar lines. 'I think I should go up and see if my dad is there,' he whispered, pointing up at the ridge.

'I'll go with you,' said David.

★   ★   ★

David and Paulie got to the rocks without any trouble. The moon was bright enough to give them some idea of their position.

Paulie pulled up his horse and sniffed. 'Wood smoke,' he said.

'From our camp, do you think?' said David, looking back across the plain, where their own camp-fires were visible.

'No, it's round here somewhere,' said Paulie, 'I'm sure.' He stopped talking, held up his hand and pointed. There was a slight glow over one of the rocks. He was right, someone close by had lit a fire.

Both men dismounted, pulled their

guns and crept towards the dim light. They were young and nimble enough to get to the top of the rock silently and peer over. There was the campfire, glowing redly. A horse was tethered nearby; David saw that it was Caleb's. Sitting by the fire, stirring a pot that hung over it was a figure, clearly recognizable as Sheriff Layton la Bute.

David glanced at Paulie and nodded. Both men cocked their pistols and ran down the slope. David let off a shot as la Bute looked up and went for his rifle, which was lying by the fire, but realizing they meant business, he jerked upright and remained immobile as the men approached him. Paulie retrieved the rifle and went to the horse and took the gun-belt that hung from the pommel of the saddle.

'Where's the rest?' asked David.

'Rest of what?' said la Bute.

'MacPherson's men.'

La Bute shrugged and leaned forward. David took a step closer, keeping his gun steady.

'I was just going to move my pot from the fire,' said la Bute, 'before my vittles burn.' David kicked the pan off the fire.

'Are you expecting me to believe my dad sent you here on your own?' asked Paulie.

'Your dad,' spat la Bute, 'kicked me out of town, on account of me being let down by his no-good son.'

'That must have pained you greatly, la Bute,' said David. 'How much gold have you got hidden in the jailhouse?'

He saw la Bute's eyes narrow. 'None of your business.'

'It surely is, since you killed my grandpa to get it,' said David.

La Bute snorted. 'Stupid old feller should have kept his flappy mouth shut.'

David cocked his pistol.

'Steady, friend,' said Paulie.

David nodded. 'It's all right, I ain't going to kill him.'

'Why did you try to stampede the herd?' asked Paulie.

La Bute giggled. 'Didn't try, son, I succeeded. How many head did you lose?'

'Nowhere near enough to cause us a problem,' said David.

'I saw you nearly bought it, though. That would have cheered me up no end, sending you off to meet dear old grandpa in the happy hunting grounds.'

Paulie took a step closer to him now. 'That's enough, la Bute. Why do you want to ruin us?'

La Bute was still laughing. 'Pure spite. I was up on Mint Creek, hoping to retrieve what I can from the situation, since my plans have been so ruined by your interference. Then I came across your rotten outfit, and I thought, why not? Any trouble I can cause you gives me pleasure.'

'Get a rope, Paulie,' said David. 'Seems like I'm going to be adding to your bad luck, Sheriff. You're going with us back to Clearwater Springs, where Marshal Sykes is waiting to arrest you, then you'll stand trial for the murder of my grandfather.'

La Bute looked unimpressed. 'Nothing can ever be proved, it'll just be your word against mine, breed. And anyway, I ain't going back to Clearwater, so there'll be no arrest.'

Paulie had returned with the rope from la Bute's horse. 'Hold out your hands,' he ordered.

In a flash la Bute reached behind him and pulled a knife from his belt. Paulie wasn't anywhere near quick enough and he jerked and shuddered as la Bute twisted the blade in his stomach. David let off a couple of shots, but Paulie was too close for him to get a good aim. La Bute pulled out the knife and snatched up a rifle, which Paulie had dropped, and scampered backwards to his horse, firing a couple of shots as he leapt aboard. David emptied his revolver, but la Bute had already made good his escape.

David dropped to his knees next to Paulie, who was writhing on the ground, blood, jet-black in the firelight, oozing across his stomach. David took his friend's hands and placed them against the wound. 'Keep pressing, Paulie,' he said. 'I'm gonna get you back to camp.'

Paulie began to scream as he pulled him up the rocks. 'Shoot me, Davy,' he sobbed. 'I'm done for.'

'Keep pressing,' shouted David. 'Don't give up.'

They tumbled down the other side, and Paulie briefly passed out. Both men were slippery with blood as David managed to get his friend into the saddle. His agonized groaning indicating that painful consciousness was returning. 'Keep pressing!' was David's constant refrain. 'I'm going to get you back to the camp.'

13

Mark's anger was so great he lost control and grabbed his son, shook him thoroughly then hurled him down to the ground. 'You damn blasted arrogant fool of a boy!' he screamed. 'Why can you never take any advice you're given? Thanks to you Paulie's likely to die, and for what?'

David tried to get up, but his father's boot in his ribs knocked him back again.

Mark continued his rant. 'You could both have been killed! Now I'm a hand down and la Bute's still running round the countryside full of hate for us.'

David sat up and grunted, holding his side. 'La Bute don't need any help to hate, and anyway, he's running back to Mint Creek to try and get more gold. He ain't going to bother you or your precious herd.' He managed to pull himself upright without any interference this time. 'And Mint Creek is where I'm headed. La Bute admitted he'd killed Grandpa and I've got to bring him to justice.'

Mark lashed out at David again, but this time David was ready for him and sidestepped him neatly. 'You'll have to manage without me, and I have to get la Bute. Don't you understand I can't let him get away with murder? The murder of your wife's father, remember.'

Mark was panting heavily, from frustration more than exertion. 'Don't you dare mention your mother to me! It would have broken her heart to see what you've become.'

'It would have broken her heart if I let the murderer of her father get away with it. If I leave now I've got a good chance of tracking la Bute down.'

'Damn and blast you, son.' Mark waved his arms ineffectually. 'Go, leave, and I don't care if you come back or not. You go and play at being a US marshal, since getting these cows through Mint Falls Canyon clearly ain't interesting enough for you.'

David picked up his hat and knocked the dust off it. He said no more to his father and walked towards the chuck wagon.

Paulie had been put on the table Olly used to prepare the food. Some of the hands were holding lanterns over him, so Olly could see what he was doing.

Caroline came over to him, wiping her damp hands on a piece of cloth. 'He's not dead yet, that's all I can say, though Olly thinks the bleeding has stopped. You're covered in blood. Find a change of clothes and leave those with me.'

He looked down, only then realizing, in the lamplight, how stained he was. 'Yes,' he said. He looked back at her. 'Aren't you going to tell me what a damn fool I've been?'

'I'm sure your father has been eloquent on the matter. You did what you thought was right, you always do.'

She sounded so sad and tired.

'And now I'm going to ride to Mint Creek and apprehend Layton la Bute.'

She looked away. 'That's the right thing to do, I suppose.'

'He's admitted killing Grandpa.'

'Change your clothes before you go or you'll have buzzards trailing you all the way to the Creek.'

'Caro . . . '

She looked up at him. 'Yes?'

'Do you think I'm an arrogant fool?' He saw the hint of a smile dimple the corners of her mouth.

'Sometimes, but aren't we all?'

$$\star \quad \star \quad \star$$

Mint Creek had been a favourite haunt of Dancing Bird. He said it was good for hunting and had taken his grandson there many times. David pondered over recent events as he let his horse walk at a steady pace, waiting for the sun to rise before he picked up some speed. He wondered what his father had meant when, thinking they were under attack from MacPherson, he said it was personal. Had that been significant? David knew from past experience that his family kept things from him. They only let him know his mother was ill when her condition became desperate and he got back just in time to be with her when she died.

That was when he met Dancing Bird. His grandparents had disowned his mother when she married a white man and took on his ways, but after his wife died, Dancing Bird had sought and been given forgiveness, and been taken on as one of the family at River Bow Ranch. Something else that no one had thought to tell David while he'd been in Vermont. Their excuse was that his mother had been determined that nothing would jeopardize his career at the bank, of which she was immensely proud.

Dancing Bird had, in his grudgingly curmudgeonly way, taken to David and even though they often exasperated each other, David became fond of his grandfather. It was during the time he had spent at River Bow, after his mother's death, that David had often gone to Mint Creek with the old man.

Visibility was improving by the second, David spurred on his horse and soon he was steadily cantering along the trail.

* * *

The prospectors' tatty encampment spoiled the charm of the bubbling creek and the verdant vegetation around it. A true oasis amidst the arid terrain. As David arrived he saw two wagons being loaded, ready to leave.

'Wasting your time, son,' said one man, as he hauled a bag up the tail gate. 'No gold here, I promise you.'

'I know,' said David, 'I'm after a man.' He described la Bute and his horse.

The prospector shrugged. 'I did hear someone go through the camp in the night and at something of a lick, but this is a coming and going place, I took no notice.'

The owner of the adjoining wagon told a similar story, and all that David could ascertain was that the rider was heading downstream. David, too, followed the course of the twinkling water. He tried to think where the gold might be. It was someplace where a grappling iron and a rope were needed. He remembered Dancing Bird used a nearby cave when he stayed overnight, so he headed there first.

Someone else had used the cave as a shelter. Inside was the remains of a camp-fire and some empty cans had been thrown to the rear. It was only a short cave and there didn't seem to be any crevices or passages where gold could be hidden. But David couldn't get the idea of caves out of his mind, as his grandfather always seemed rather keen on them. Then he remembered what Dancing Bird had said about the cave hidden behind the waterfall.

Having no other lead, David decided to follow the creek as far as he could.

Away from the camp the scene was idyllic. The crystal water tumbled tunefully over the rocky bed, and birds sang and flew between the trees in a small copse. In the distance he could hear the louder splash as the creek became the narrow waterfall. David tethered his tired horse, and walked stealthily along the path. The trees were replaced by scrubby shrubs on the plateau before the canyon. He stopped short as he heard the soft whinny of a horse. Not his own. He crept a few more paces and then, behind a clump of thorny vegetation he saw Caleb's bay. He went over and ran his hand along its neck. It nudged him gently. La Bute could not be far away. David walked along the edge of the plateau, where the water frothed white and spray misted the air. There was no path down into the valley below. Then he saw a rope twisted round a solid boulder, with the grappling hook firmly wedged into the

225

ground. The rope snaked over the edge, and David tentatively peered into the chasm. There was no one to be seen. So it seemed his grandfather had been right; there must be a cave in the cliff face. How the robbers had found it and got the gold to such an inaccessible place, David could not imagine, and it must have been a million to one chance that Dancing Bird had discovered it. At least he knew now what he had to do. He went back to Caleb's horse. There were already two ingots in the saddle-bag. David was dog tired, so la Bute must be on the verge of complete exhaustion if he was lugging gold up a sheer rock face. David loosened the girth to the saddle, found himself a comfortable spot in the scrubby area, sat down, pulled his gun and waited.

It wasn't long before he saw the rope twitching, and heard the loud panting of a man. La Bute pulled himself untidily over the edge, throwing a heavy bag in front of him. He stood up and coughed, holding his sides as he did so. He picked up the bag and headed for his horse. He swore loudly as the saddle slipped over under the weight of the gold. David stepped into the clearing and cocked his gun. 'Stay right where you are, la Bute,' he said. 'You're under arrest for the murder of Dancing Bird — '

La Bute attempted to draw, but David discharged a chamber. La Bute span round. David, being no great shot, wondered if he'd actually hit him, but when la Bute recovered his balance, he was holding his thigh, which was stained red.

'Just a scratch, breed,' he panted.

'Throw your gun over,' said David, 'take it out gently now.'

'You some sort of law man now are you, breed?'

'Gun, please,' said David.

'Nah,' said la Bute with a sly smile. 'You're too decent to shoot me, you ain't got the — '

David let off another shot, which slammed into the ground and left la Bute hopping around. 'I don't mind if I save the hangman the trouble,' said David. 'I know you did it, so you're a dead man whatever I do.'

La Bute snorted, then was forced back to his awkward dance as David fired off another shot.

David raised his eyebrows. 'Give me your gun. If you manage to escape from me, the Apache will track you down. I've let them know you murdered one of their own,' he lied, 'and what they're going to do to you is worse than any hangman. All in all, you're better off coming with me.'

La Bute was no fool. If David had managed to inform the Indians about his guilt, he probably would be better off standing trial, or at least staying with David until some opportunity to escape presented itself. So he threw over his gun.

'Tighten up the girths, la Bute,' said David, 'you're coming with me.'

'What about my injury?' whined la Bute.

'Just a scratch, ain't it?'

* * *

On reaching the herd David put la Bute in Tom's custody and made straight for the chuck wagon. Much to his surprise Paulie was propped up in the back, conscious and lucid, though he looked deathly pale.

David's smile was broad. 'Well I can't deny I've seen better-looking shit, but you're a sight for sore eyes, Paulie.'

Even smiling caused Paulie to wince. 'I feel just like you'd imagine you would when you've had your guts knifed,' he croaked. 'It ain't certain, but Olly says I might make it.'

'You hold him to that.'

'I'd be a darn sight better if I didn't have to endure all this bumping,' said Paulie.

'Quit complaining, I'm taking the smooth route,' Olly's voice shouted back down the wagon. 'Best you go and find your pa, Young Boss. He's been fretting about you something terrible, now Miss Caroline's persuaded him not to kill you.'

* * *

'That's all we need, a bound prisoner,' said Mark, his scowl almost hiding the expression of relief that had spread over his face since he saw his son.

'It's good la Bute will be held to account for his crimes, though,' said Caroline.

'There's a time and place,' said Mark. 'Undoubtedly la Bute should swing for what he's done, but we're getting close to the canyon now, and we could have trouble getting these cows through. I could do without the bother of the man.'

'I'll get back to work, Pa,' said David.

'When did you last sleep?' asked Caroline. 'You look pretty bad.'

'I'll sleep well enough once we're back at River Bow.'

* * *

After the canyon was negotiated, all that was left was the last piece of desert to cross. As the moon was so much fuller, they managed to drive the whole night through, and then let the cows jog happily towards the river. By daybreak the air smelt of mud as after a mad scramble the herd got to the water and were drinking their fill.

Mark, at last, looked content. He smiled at his son. 'I'll tell the hands to get them to the pastures once they've finished here. I need to get back to Clearwater Springs and make sure everything's all right at the bank.'

'Sure, Pa, and I need to get Paulie to the doctor and Layton la Bute into Marshal Sykes' custody. We'll bring Caroline with us as well. Since la Bute's owned up to Grandpa's murder, Caleb's off the hook, so she can go back East with Hunter, as he'll no longer be needed. All in all it's worked out well, I'm happier thinking of her travelling that distance with someone.'

'Hmm,' said Mark, 'if that's the way you're determined to play it.' He called all the hands over. 'Tom, Flynn, Caleb, Stumpy and Louisa, are you five all right taking these cows over to the pastures without us?'

'Think we can manage that, Boss, can't we?' said Tom with a grin, all the others nodded their agreement.

'Right, the rest of us are headed to town. Olly, you get Paulie to the doctor at the safest pace you can, eh? We'll meet you there.'

'Sure thing, Boss,' said Olly. 'The boy's doing better than I thought, we'll see you in town.'

'I'll buy you all a beer,' Paulie's voice drifted from the back of the wagon.

'I'll look forward to that, son,' said Mark.

'I can help move the herd,' said Caroline.

'You're coming with us,' said David.

Not realizing his intentions she acquiesced without any argument.

They forded the river and kept a steady canter towards the track that would eventually lead to the River Bow

Ranch and then Clearwater Springs. La Bute narrowed his eyes. He would have to make his move soon; the last thing he wanted was to make the acquaintance of this Marshal Sykes. He pulled on the ropes that tied his hands to the pommel of the saddle. They were disappointingly firm.

David looked at him. 'Three of us, one of you, you'll never make good your escape,' he said, as if he could read his mind.

'I only see two men. The other one's a little lady who's not armed and unlikely to be able to stop me,' grinned la Bute.

'I would consider it my duty to do everything to apprehend you, since you'd be a fugitive from justice,' she said firmly.

La Bute laughed some more. 'Now of the three of you, I'd most like to see you, miss, try and stop me.'

'Shut your face, la Bute,' said David. 'You save your mindless yakking for the trial judge.'

'Trial, what trial,' he sniggered under his breath.

★ ★ ★

They were now on the familiar track that led home. They passed the stable block where Dancing Bird had been found. As they rounded the corner what wasn't so familiar was the line of gunmen who blocked their further progress.

David's horse reared as bullets slammed into the ground in front of him. They all pulled their mounts to a juddering halt. MacPherson, who was in the middle of the line, nudged his horse towards them.

'Just a friendly warning that you're trespassing on MacPherson land,' he said with a triumphant smile. 'Now, if you want to pass through and on your way, that's fine, my boys will see you off *my* property.'

'We've paid off the loan, MacPherson,' said David, 'as you well know. You and your 'boys' go back to your own ranch and we'll say no more, eh.'

MacPherson shook his head. 'No payment's been made that I'm aware of, so today being the first of the month I took possession, as I'm entitled to.'

'We had a banker's draft. Our attorney, Hunter F. Dutton, brought it with him on the stage,' said Mark. 'Don't tell me the stage didn't get through.'

'Stage arrived on time,' said MacPherson. 'If there was someone called Hunter, or whatever, on it, he never made it to the bank.'

Caroline's heart beat fast. 'What have you done with Hunter, you wicked man!' she shouted.

MacPherson ignored her.

'Your son was almost killed on the trail. He'll be here soon and we need to get him to the doctor. You must let him pass,' she said.

'Since I ain't got no son I don't understand what you're saying, but I'm happy to let you and your sick through,

235

just as long as you don't bother me none.'

'Paulie, your son, damn near died and still could do,' said David. 'You can't disown him just like that.'

'You passing through or are you going to cause trouble?' asked MacPherson.

Mark turned to his companions and indicated they should ride away from MacPherson, which they did, pulling up out of his earshot. 'This ain't your quarrel, Caroline,' said Mark. 'I suggest you carry on and make your way to town. La Bute, I couldn't care less what happens to him.' He lowered his voice to talk to David and Caroline. 'Davy, this man's stolen my ranch, I reckon I've got to make trouble. I'll respect you whether you stay with me or not, but I'd rather you left.'

'One or two of you can't stand up to this lot,' gasped Caroline, 'and you mustn't even think of doing so. We should all go to town, find the marshal and try to discover what's happened to Hunter.'

Mark turned down his lips. 'Reckon I've been trying to do things the right way for too long. I gotta stand up to this man at some time, might as well be now.'

'Pa,' said David, 'I want to whup MacPherson's ass just as much as you do, but Caro's got a point. Us two against twenty or so armed men, it would be suicide.'

Mark's lips were set in a firm line. 'I know it ain't sensible, but I've gone as far as I'm prepared to go with MacPherson.'

'All right,' conceded David, 'but, even if you ain't prepared to go to town, we should say that's what we're doing, to get through the line. Caro, you hightail it out of here as fast as you can; we'll make for the ranch house. At least we'll have some cover there, and if they haven't ransacked the place, more guns and ammunition.'

'I still don't think that's good

enough,' said Caroline. 'Please be sensible, don't die over a few square miles of land.'

'I can't hear what you're saying! What you planning? You gotta cut me free,' whined la Bute. Everyone ignored him.

'I'm going to my house,' said Mark. 'You two head off.'

David reached out and grasped Caroline's hand. 'I gotta stay with pa.'

She nodded, swallowing hard and making no attempt to hide the tears that ran down her cheeks. 'I'll get what help I can.' She looked at Mark. 'Please,' she whispered. 'Don't die like this.'

'Ain't planning on dying, Caroline, I'm planning on getting my ranch back once and for all.' Mark rode back towards MacPherson. 'You'll let us through this line so we can make our way to town?'

'As long as that's what you do, I'll let you go. You deviate from the track I'll cut you down like dogs.'

La Bute was panic-stricken and was

wriggling violently in the saddle. 'Untie me,' he screamed. 'I ain't getting mixed up in no range war. MacPherson, I've got gold in my saddlebags and hidden in your jail. You untie me now, I'll make you a rich man.'

'I'm already rich,' laughed MacPherson.

La Bute was practically vibrating in the saddle. 'You ain't that rich! No one's that rich. I'm talking real gold ingots, come and see.' His struggling with his bonds was now so extreme that his horse began to toss its head and to skitter about beneath him.

'You do what you want with him,' Mark called to MacPherson, seeing that la Bute was causing something of a diversion. 'Let us through and we'll be out of your hair.'

'Ingots?' MacPherson was saying as he waved his arm, indicating his men should part. He tried to reach up to take the reins of la Bute's horse, but the animal, already nervous, jinxed back from him.

'Now,' said Mark.

They spurred their horses through and kept to the track and then sharply veered off and galloped towards the house. Then they heard gunfire, just making it to the protection of the rear of the house in time. They stumbled through the back door into the kitchen. Mark immediately pulled the heavy table across the door; David dashed into the hall and pulled the sideboard there in front of the main door.

'At least we shuttered the downstairs windows before we left,' he said, as they heard bullets slamming into the wood.

'Get away from the door,' cried Mark, snatching Caroline out of danger as the planks splintered and a shot ricocheted off the floor.

'Thought you were going to town,' said David, breathlessly.

'Didn't seem such a good plan, when people started shooting at us.'

Mark pulled open the door to the hall cupboard and snatched out a couple of rifles and some boxes of ammunition. 'Upstairs,' he said.

'What do we do now?' said Caroline, as David grabbed her hand and pulled her up the staircase.

'Dunno,' he said truthfully. 'Looks like we've got ourselves into a siege situation.'

14

Caroline stepped away from the window and began to shake, the gun she held in her hand clattered to the floor.

Mark took a few more shots then went over to her. 'Sit on the bed,' he said kindly. 'There, there.' He pushed her gently against the pillows as her eyes began to glaze. 'Davy, Davy, in here, quick.'

Gunfire continued to crack outside. He went back to the window and let off more rifle shots, then searched frantically inside the wardrobe, which he had pushed nearly right across the window, leaving only a crack, through which he could shoot. 'There you are,' he muttered at last as he retrieved the bottle of whiskey.

'Caro!' cried David as he rushed into the room. 'Are you hurt?'

She blinked her eyes rapidly when she saw him. 'Never thought I'd hit anyone,' she croaked.

Mark pulled out the cork with his teeth, and thrust the bottle into her hand. 'Take it straight from the neck, girl, you're doing well.'

She nodded and obeyed him.

'How you doing, son?' asked Mark.

'Winged a couple, I think. Hell, Pa, I've no desire to kill anyone.'

Caroline coughed and held out the bottle. David took it from her and helped himself to a hefty swig. 'It'll be dark in a few hours, Pa. They'll be sure to try something then.'

Mark sighed, taking the bottle from his son. 'Yeah, reckon they will.'

The brief quiet outside was punctuated once more by the sound of gunshot. David went up to the window this time to return fire. Then he returned to the bed and sat next to Caroline, who, though still shaking, looked rather better than she had a few minutes before.

He rubbed his face with his hands. 'We're relatively safe here, they'd have to be dammed lucky to hit any of us, but we are stuck.'

'They'll have to starve us out,' said Mark.

'Or burn,' said Caroline hoarsely. 'There's a lot of wood on this house — that's what I'd do, burn it.'

David let out a long breath. 'One, let's hope they ain't as clever as you. Two, let's hope MacPherson wants the house for himself.'

'I don't think he'll be bothered by the house,' said Mark, 'but don't forget, our hands will be back eventually. They should be able to help us.'

'I wish we could warn them,' said Caroline. 'They'll be in danger too.'

Mark started to pace the room. 'Davy, Caroline, I apologize,' he said. 'I call you a damned arrogant fool when you don't listen to the advice I give you, Davy, and today I behaved just the same way. You're right, we should have gone to town, but MacPherson got me so riled, I wasn't prepared to back down.'

'Like son, like father, eh,' said David with a smile.

'Connor MacPherson is a very bad man,' said Caroline. 'I wouldn't have trusted him not to shoot us in the back.'

They all paused.

'Mighty quiet,' said Mark.

David peeped out of the window. 'They're just standing there, down by the bunkhouse in a huddle. Wonder how much ammunition they've got. Maybe we should draw their fire.'

'I'm happy for a minute's breather,' said Mark, handing the bottle back to Caroline.

David thought for a while. 'Why don't you think MacPherson wants this house, Pa? Is there something we should know?'

Mark shrugged. 'Not really.'

Caroline frowned. 'Mark, if there's something that helps explain this situation, don't you think you should tell us?'

'Well, I dunno.'

'Pa!' exclaimed David. 'Just how personal is this? What happened between you and Connor MacPherson? Maybe we could do something about it.'

'I don't think so,' sighed Mark. 'All right, Connor did threaten to ruin me over something I did.' He took another deep breath. 'After your ma died, when you went back to Vermont and I sent Lou to another school, well, Bessie, you know, Connor's wife, she took to coming over here, making sure I was all right, bringing me food and such.'

'Pa, you didn't!' cried David, his voice sharp with disapproval.

'Course I didn't,' snapped Mark. 'But I got to talking to her. She was always a quiet person, but she started to open up to me. She started to tell me about her life with Connor.'

David pursed his lips; things were slotting into place in his mind. 'He was beating her, right?'

Caroline gasped.

Mark looked surprised. 'You knew?'

'No, but Paulie told me once his pa had beat him.'

Mark nodded. 'From what Bessie told me, he'd been using her badly almost from the start. She put up with it because she had to.'

'No one has to put up with being beaten!' said Caroline.

'How could she get away?' said Mark as if that explained everything. 'That weren't the worst of it. You know we'd always been told Paulie's sister was a cripple due to a riding accident? Not true. The girl caught her pa thumping Bessie hard and tried to intervene. He threw her down the stairs.'

'The brute!' said Caroline. 'Why don't we just shoot him down?'

'Anyway,' concluded Mark, 'Bessie had a sister in Texas she could go to, so I got her and the girl on the stage and went with them to Carlyle, and made sure they got the train. When he found out I'd helped them escape, Connor vowed to ruin me, but I was alone then, missing Mary more than I could have thought possible. I didn't care about anything but blocking it all out with as much drink as I could stomach. Then Lou got expelled from school, again, and she tried to sort things out. Well, you know the rest.'

David bit his lip. 'Ain't nothing we can say or do that's going to pacify Connor, is there? I'm surprised it's taken him this long.'

'Oh, I think he's enjoyed drawing it out,' said Mark.

David went back to the window. 'They're lighting a fire,' he said over his shoulder. 'Makes sense. They'll either try to burn us out or create a diversion at the front, while they attempt to get in at the back. Dammit, Pa, why d'you build this house so big?'

'Me and your ma planned to breed us a tribe all of our own. Don't know why it stopped with Lou, it wasn't for want of trying.'

'Pa!' said David, his lip curling with distaste.

'Just answering your question.'

Caroline got up and retrieved the gun she had dropped from the floor. 'So, it seems to me, we've got to concentrate on killing MacPherson. Once he's gone the hired gunslingers won't be bothered to stay on, will they?'

David frowned. 'I can't believe Miss Caroline Fisher of Waverley, Vermont said that. It's true, though, and guess who never comes in range of our guns?'

'A brute and a coward, then,' she said.

There was a crashing noise and the sound of a horse neighing from the rear of the house. Taking his rifle and keeping his head down, David raced across the landing. He was soon back. 'La Bute's being dragged round the vegetable garden by his horse.'

'He's still tied on?' asked Mark.

'Just about,' said David. 'There's no sign of MacPherson's men at the back. I don't really know what to do about la Bute. I'd hate to lose him.'

'Don't think about bringing him in, son,' said Mark. 'Like as not they've set him up as a trap to flush us out.'

Caroline was peering out of the window. 'They're coming towards the house with torches now,' she said, shakily trying to aim her gun.

The sound of gunfire filled the air, the short crack of hand guns, together with the longer echoing report of rifle fire.

Caroline grappled with the gun, trying to steady it by using both hands. David gently pulled her away from the window. 'Leave this to me,' he said, poking the barrel of his rifle out.

'My hands are all shaky and slippy. I can't do this,' she cried.

''Course you can't,' said David. 'Now keep back.' He let off a shot.

'Got one!' shouted Mark.

'Wasn't me,' said David, 'I was miles off.'

'Wasn't me,' said Mark. 'Hell, they're falling like skittles. What in tarnation's going on?'

Caroline looked over David's shoulder. Three men lay motionless on the ground before the house. The other men were running back towards the bunkhouse, their flaming torches discarded on the ground. MacPherson stood by the bunkhouse door, gesticulating wildly for his men to turn around. She could hear shouting but could not make out what anyone was saying. A single shot rang out, MacPherson span round, and sprawled on the floor.

'We've got help,' she said.

'The others must be back,' said David, trying to get a better look, but still unwilling to put his head out of the window.

MacPherson's hands gathered around him. Within minutes two more of them came into view, leading the horses. David let off some shots, just to keep them nervous, but they were way out of his range and they knew it.

'MacPherson must be dead,' said Caroline, as some of the men mounted.

But she was wrong, as they saw him, clutching his shoulder, but standing, being helped onto his horse. Another couple of shots echoed across the yard. No one seemed to be hit and the men all galloped away.

'Was that all of them?' shouted Mark.

'Yep!' said David. 'Counted them out.'

Without saying any more he and his father ran out of the bedroom and clattered down the stairs.

By the time Caroline got outside, her progress rather slow as her legs were wobbly, she could see Olly's wagon perched up on the hillside. As she watched she saw it begin to trundle down. David was hunched down next to one of the dead men. He looked up at her.

She smiled weakly. 'That was Paulie shooting the wings off a gnat,' she said, swallowing hard, trying to stop the tears that threatened to cascade down her face.

'Fancy shooting indeed,' said David.

Olly was grim-faced when he finally pulled up his wagon before the ranch house.

'Not before time, Olly,' said Mark, smiling broadly. 'We thought we were stuck in there for the duration.'

Olly jumped down from the driving seat and went to the back and lifted up the flap. 'He insisted,' he said. 'Reckoned he was the only man he knew who could pick those men off at that distance. And he did.' Olly's voice cracked.

Caroline looked into the back of the wagon. Paulie lay flat on his back, deathly pale. She gripped Olly's arm. 'What happened?' she whispered.

'Told him not to do it,' said Olly. 'He wasn't even half healed. I knew the effort would open the wound, but he wouldn't be stopped.' He dropped his head in respect. 'In the end there was just too much blood, I couldn't save him.'

'He died saving our lives,' she managed to croak before the tears, which had threatened for so long, burst out in a hot, uncontrollable gush. She felt strong arms enfold her and knew it was David as she buried her face in his chest.

'It's all right,' he said, sniffing loudly himself. 'You cry if you want.'

Mark's fist shot out and slammed into the side of the wagon. 'Damn, blast that man!' he raged. 'MacPherson might as well have held a gun to his son's head and shot him himself.'

*　*　*

'If you don't untie me, little lady, I'm going to piss my pants,' screamed la Bute. David had rescued him from the vegetable garden, where his terrified horse had backed itself into a corner, with la Bute hanging helpless from the pommel. David had brought him inside and tied him to the banister rail in the hall.

Caroline looked at him as she came out of the kitchen doorway. 'I can't release you, Mr la Bute,' she said. 'But out of a humanitarian spirit, I'll call David and see if he'll take you to — '

'You hurry up, little lady, or you're going to have a load of laundry and mopping up to do.'

'There's no need to be so graphic, Mr la Bute,' she said and went outside.

David and his father were tying the bodies of MacPherson's men onto their horses. David, rightly she thought, had not wanted to take them into town next to Paulie, who still lay in the chuck wagon.

Olly was coming up the steps to the house. 'I'm going to ride out and tell the others what's happened,' he said.

'There's hot bacon, beans and coffee in the kitchen. Have something to eat before you go,' she said.

'Surely will, miss,' said Olly, removing his hat and going inside.

'I'm hungry and thirsty too,' whined la Bute.

'One thing at a time, sir,' Caroline shouted back at him, as she went down the steps.

David smiled at her. 'You look better, how are you feeling?'

'Better. Odd, really weird, but better. Do you understand?'

'Yes I do. I'm so proud — ' He stopped short, swallowed hard, then frowned. 'Why is la Bute screaming?'

'That's why I came to you. He's begging me to let him use the lavatory.'

David raised his eyebrows slightly. 'It's probably best if I allow him to do that. I'll be along in a while.'

'I think it's pretty urgent,' she said. He followed her back into the house. She heard him warning la Bute to make no attempt to escape as she went back into the kitchen.

Olly was wiping up the remains of his food with some bread. 'Mighty welcome, miss,' he said, using the last of the slice to wipe his mouth.

She suddenly felt very shaky again and dropped into the chair next to Olly.

He chuckled. 'Reckon you need some of this as much as us,' he said, ladling out a portion.

'I thought I was better.'

'You will be when you eat.'

She shook her head, but Olly pretty much pushed a forkful into her mouth and she began to chew. Now she needed more.

'Olly!' she heard David's voice. 'You still there?'

Olly went out and she heard him laugh. 'He had to try then, Young Boss?'

'And I had to knock him out. Help me drag him back in.'

Mark walked past them, cocking an eyebrow as the prone la Bute was pulled across the polished wood floor. He shook his head. 'Even unconscious that man annoys me.' He helped himself to some food and sat next to Caroline. 'I suggest you and I go to town in the wagon with Paulie. I'll let David bring in la Bute and the bodies.'

She nodded.

'This is good,' said Mark, indicating

the food. 'Let's hope this high-fandanging marshal that David seems to have such faith in will take la Bute off our hands.'

'What about MacPherson?' she asked.

'He needs to come and see Paulie and make sure the boy gets a decent burial at the least. Things got out of hand today. Something needs to be done about this feud; I don't want any more lives lost.'

'I agree,' she said with feeling.

'You all right to come into town?' he asked. 'I'd rather you did, I don't like the idea of leaving you here alone.'

'I want to go to town. At the very least we need to find out what happened to Hunter.'

'Bet you really want to go home now, don't you. And just when David seems to be treating you with a bit of affection at last.'

She studied the wood grain in the table. 'He's always there when I'm upset, when I need him,' she said softly.

'But he'll back off again.' She looked at Mark. 'I was frightened today. Scared I would die, scared I would kill someone, scared I would kill and be pleased I'd done it. Vermont is a peaceful, beautiful place. Everything here is so — intense. But there are so many people here that I love.' She took a shuddering breath. 'I think it'll be a while before I can think straight about anything.'

'Yeah,' said Mark softly. 'Much as I'd like you to stay, maybe Davy is right.' He reached out and gripped her hand. 'This is one hard, tough country. I'd hate to see you hurt.'

She squeezed his hand back. 'Let's do what we've got to do today, shall we? The rest can wait.'

15

Twilight was just settling around them as they trundled into Clearwater Springs. David intended to go straight to the jail with la Bute and the corpses of MacPherson's men, while Mark and Caroline went to the undertaker with Paulie. However, a group of people congregating outside the jailhouse made them all stop there.

'I'm looking for Marshal Sykes,' called David. 'Is he here?'

The people spoke quickly amongst themselves.

'We should let them out,' he heard a woman say.

'Have you seen Connor MacPherson today, Mr Merkel?' said a tall balding man to Mark.

'I have, Pastor Sims,' said Mark. 'And he was hell bent on killing me.'

Sims looked surprised.

'And I've got the body of Paulie here in the wagon. The boy died saving our lives.'

The small crowd gasped.

'What's going on?' asked David.

'Maybe you better come inside,' said the pastor. 'I take it you know Marshal Sykes?'

'Only by name.' David dismounted. 'I've got a prisoner here needs putting behind bars. And the bodies of three dead men who were hired by MacPherson to take our ranch.'

'Sheriff la Bute,' said Sims, looking up at David's companion. 'Mr MacPherson said we were to have no more to do with him.'

'That's about the only decent thing MacPherson's ever said.' David pulled the protesting la Bute off his horse. 'Thought you'd be pleased to be back with your gold,' he whispered in his ear.

The crowd, which included the blacksmith and the undertaker, parted as David and his prisoner followed the pastor. 'You see,' said the clergyman, 'there's been a bit of a situation at the jail but without Mr MacPherson, well, we've not really been able to resolve anything.'

Mark frowned. 'Reckon I'm going in too.'

Caroline slipped down from the seat of the wagon and followed him inside. 'Hunter!' she cried, rushing to the bars of the cell which contained three men, one of them the attorney. 'Hunter!' she reached through the bars and he took her hand. 'Hunter, dear Lord! What has happened to your face?'

'Mr MacPherson pistol whipped him,' said one of the other men. 'I tried to stop him, but it's difficult. Mr MacPherson, well, he might as well own me.'

'Is one of you gentlemen a Mr David Merkel?' boomed the voice of the third man.

'Yes, that's me,' said David. 'You must be Marshal Elijah Sykes.' He looked around the room. 'Who's got the keys? None of these men should be in jail. Mr Carson, you know, is your bank manager, the other man is our attorney, Hunter Dutton and this is Marshal Sykes from Carlyle.'

'Mr MacPherson's got the key,' said the blacksmith. 'I've got the tools to release these men. It didn't seem right they were locked up, but Mr MacPherson said they were bank robbers and we were to leave them there until he got the real marshal. None of us have known what to do. I mean, Mr Carson ain't a bank robber is he? And the man who says he's the marshal has got a badge and all.'

'That's because I *am* the marshal,' boomed Sykes.

'Let them out,' said David. 'MacPherson's lost his mind, to put it kindly. Can you cut through these bars?'

The blacksmith shook what looked like a bunch of twisted wires. 'No need, I can pick the lock with these. I'm just worried I'm going against MacPherson. I mean he owns the forge.'

'Use your sense, man,' said Hunter. 'I was here to do legitimate business with Mr Carson, not rob his bank. MacPherson's only a rancher isn't he? Why are you all in such thrall to him?'

''Cos he owns most of them,' said David under his breath.

'I'll take responsibility,' said Pastor Sims. 'You release these men, Richard. Any trouble with Mr MacPherson, I'll say I told you to do it.'

The blacksmith nodded, and twisted his wires in the lock, which soon clicked open. Hunter, Carson and Sykes burst out and everyone started talking at once.

'Can you do that trick in reverse, Richard?' David asked the blacksmith, who nodded. With great relief David pushed la Bute into the cell and it was with satisfaction he heard the mechanism of the lock fall back into place.

The pastor was trying to restore some sort of order. David saw that Hunter and Caroline had retreated to a corner and he quickly joined them.

'Did MacPherson do this to you?' David asked.

'What an appalling man,' said Hunter. 'The longer people like that think they can ride roughshod over the law, and any other aspect of decent behaviour, the longer it will take for the West to be civilized.'

'What actually happened?' said David.

'I went straight to the bank when I got here, and found Carson an easy fellow to do business with, and before long all the formalities had been seen to. Then the man MacPherson burst in, which I thought was rude, but then this is Arizona and I've no idea what passes for good manners here. With hindsight I should have seen he was mad in every sense of the word. He seemed none too pleased when Carson explained who I was and that the loan had been paid and River Bow Ranch was up and running as a going concern again. Anyway, MacPherson said there was a situation in town and he needed our help. Something to do with a man impersonating a US marshal. When we got to the jail Sykes was already locked up. MacPherson had tricked him into the cell somehow. I was more than happy to vouch for Sykes, then I realized that wasn't what MacPherson wanted at all. He pulled his gun, ordered Carson and me into the cell. Like everyone else in town, Carson is frightened of MacPherson and he meekly obeyed. I protested vehemently, and got a good thrashing for my trouble. Then we were left here, until the pastor came by and heard our shouting. You say MacPherson tried to kill you?'

'He trapped us in the ranch house,' said Caroline. 'We feared for our lives for a time. Paulie saved us, but died in the effort.'

David glanced towards the cell and the brooding la Bute. 'He died because he'd been stabbed by la Bute, the former sheriff here.'

'Dear me,' said Hunter, 'and that's

the man you suspect of killing your grandfather, isn't it?'

'He's admitted as much to me.'

'Looks like he's going to swing, if we can ever get any proper law out here. Hopefully Sykes will see to that.'

'And I think you should see the doctor, Hunter,' said Caroline.

Hunter waved her concern away. 'Just a few scratches.'

Mark and Marshal Sykes had also managed to disentangle themselves from the throng and they joined Hunter, David and Caroline.

'Never mind your man there,' said the law man pointing to la Bute, 'seems I'll be arresting Connor MacPherson, for attempted murder, trespass and several other things besides. Mr Dutton, can you prove that the business concerning the River Bow ranch was concluded legally and in time?'

Hunter tapped his breast pocket. 'I made sure I picked up the papers before I left the bank. The loan to

MacPherson's bank was fully paid. The residue of the loan from the bank in Carlyle together with the money from the three investors left the account in credit. MacPherson had no grounds whatsoever to repossess the ranch.'

David frowned. 'Three investors?'

'Nehemiah Rice, myself and Horace Fisher,' said Hunter proudly.

David's lips tightened with anger as he turned to Caroline. 'You promised! Promised! Can I never — '

'Whoa, whoa!' exclaimed Hunter. 'No wonder you're such a fit young fellow the number of times a day you climb onto that high horse of yours. This has nothing to do with Caroline. Horace Fisher is my client. When I became aware of a business venture I thought was worth backing, I felt duty-bound to inform him of the opportunity as well.'

'Can people just invest like that, without the owners knowing?' asked Mark.

'Well I was doing it for your sakes,'

said Hunter, somewhat huffily.

'Right,' said Sykes. 'Since I've been incarcerated for the best part of twenty-four hours, I'm off to get myself a beer and a bite to eat. Then, first light, I'm going to the MacPherson place. Mr Merkel Junior, I've a mind to deputize you. Be ready at dawn.' He clapped his hands, and silence at last fell. 'No one leave town,' he said, loudly and sternly. 'Blacksmith, can you make a key for the locks in this jail?' Richard nodded. 'Then get onto it, man, and bring it to Deputy Merkel when it's done. There's four dead men outside. One needs treating with real good reverence, the others need something doing. Pastor Sims, I'll leave that to you. The rest of you, away!'

Nobody did leave, however, as the door burst open and Louisa, closely followed by Flynn, hurtled inside and threw herself at Mark. 'Pa! Pa!' she cried. 'What happened? We heard there was a terrible battle and Paulie died — '

'There, there,' said Mark gently.

269

'We're all right. Come on, let's go to the hotel.'

Flynn looked speechlessly at David, shaking his head.

Sykes gave Flynn a swift appraisal. 'What's your name, son?'

'Er, Flynn, sir.'

'Right, Mr Flynn, you're deputized too. Deputy Merkel will fill you in with what's happening. Rest of you, out!'

All Flynn could do was raise an eyebrow as the jailhouse finally emptied.

Sykes slapped Hunter on the back. 'You look as much in need of a drink and a steak as I do, my man. Shall we dine together?'

'This bucket is full!' screamed la Bute. 'I'm going to piss on the floor if you don't empty it, and I'm hungry too. You gotta feed me, you know.'

Sykes looked back at David. 'I'll leave that to you, Deputy Merkel,' he said with a sly smile.

★　★　★

David and Flynn were sitting at the table in the jailhouse office sipping whiskey and talking softly when Caroline came in with a jug of beer and some food for them.

'I'm not altogether sure what this deputizing business means,' said Flynn, filling his mouth with food.

David pulled a chair over for Caroline, and poured three glasses of beer.

'Has your prisoner quietened down?' she whispered.

'We gave him half a bottle of whiskey; he soon fell asleep after that,' said David.

'Is Lou all right?' asked Flynn.

'Yes, she's gone to bed, I think she'd worked herself up into a terrible state.'

'The way Olly told it to us, you'd all been massacred, and Lou being Lou, she didn't hang around to get the full story, she just rode straight off.'

Caroline nodded. 'Marshal Sykes is trying to get a posse together. Mark and Hunter have volunteered, Pastor Sims seems keen but I think feels he shouldn't, on account of being a man of the cloth.'

'Not much of a posse, then,' said David.

'I think most people in town would volunteer if they could be sure it would get rid of MacPherson. He's treated them all like slaves for so long, they're just so terrified of him. I think by the end of the evening Mr Carson and the blacksmith will have been persuaded to volunteer.'

'And don't forget,' said Flynn, 'I reckon the rest of the hands from the River Bow will be here by first light.'

David pushed his empty plate away, stretched his arms and wriggled his shoulders.

'When did you last sleep, either of you?' asked Caroline. 'Flynn, you might as well go back to the hotel. I'll find some blankets and make up a bed for David on that couch over there.'

Flynn didn't need to be asked twice. He gathered up the crockery and said goodnight.

David lay gratefully on the couch. He couldn't stop yawning.

'This time tomorrow it should all be sorted out,' said Caroline, soothingly, pulling the blanket up to his chin.

'Hmm,' said David. 'Can't see MacPherson coming in without a fight.'

'Shh, don't think about it, sleep.'

For once he was too tired to do anything but take her advice.

* * *

Sykes was assembling his posse outside the jailhouse when Flynn noticed dust on the horizon. 'I'd say it was quite a few riders,' he said.

'Do you think MacPherson's bringing the fight to town?' David wondered aloud.

'Wouldn't be surprised,' said Sykes.

A couple of the townspeople, who, the night before, thought ridding the town of MacPherson had been a good idea, began to slip away.

Sykes mounted. 'Weapons ready,

men? We knew it would come to this. Let's go out and meet them and hope it don't get too messy. You want to say a few words, Pastor Sims?'

Sims rammed his hat further down on his furrowed forehead. 'I'm going to get my horse and my rifle.'

'Good words, brother!' said Sykes. 'Right, men, we have the law on our side, and now we've got the Lord too.'

'I feel sick,' said Caroline.

Louisa wrapped her arms around her. 'Is it worth risking any of them for a patch of near desert and a few smelly cows?'

'No,' said Caroline. 'But I think it's gone way beyond that now.'

★ ★ ★

The posse had just passed the wooden archway on which was painted 'Clear-water Springs', when Sykes held up his hand, indicating they should stop. Individual horses were now apparent on the road ahead. He turned to Mark. 'I presume that's MacPherson and his outfit?'

'Yup,' said Mark.

'I'll ride out alone; it's only fair to give the man a chance to come quietly.'

'I don't recommend that, Marshal,' said David. 'He's as likely to shoot you before you've a chance to open your mouth.'

'Nevertheless, I'll do this properly, but boys, any sign of trouble, pile on in, and the Devil take the hindmost!' Sykes set his horse off in a controlled canter.

'I suggest we move a little closer,' said David, and the posse walked their horses briskly after Sykes.

MacPherson, his left arm in a sling, galloped up and brought his horse snorting to a standstill just in front of the marshal.

'I've no quarrel with you, law man,' he said. 'Just hand over the Merkels, father and son, and I'll let you go back to Carlyle, no trouble.'

'Can't do that, Mr MacPherson,' said Sykes, 'since I'm arresting you for various crimes, most serious of which is attempted murder, followed by trespass, theft and the unlawful incarceration of three individuals, one of them this US marshal. Four men died yesterday, one of them your own son. Let's not shed any more blood, shall we, sir. Now if you'd like to follow me back to town — '

'You got this all wrong, Marshal,' said MacPherson. 'It's Merkel that's shot me and stolen from me, my land, my cows, and more, much more than that. You get yourself back to Carlyle and we'll settle this the old way. The way of the range. How's that sound to you, Mark!' He raised his voice at the end, to make sure they could all hear.

'Don't agree to that,' snapped Hunter, to Mark.

'I ain't going to,' said Mark. 'I ain't no savage. That man needs to be behind bars.'

The posse crept closer to Sykes.

Flynn let out a long breath. 'It's going to get messy, Davy. Minute it does, I'm heading for cover by that barn over there. What are you going to do?'

David bit his lip. 'Think I might throw up,' he muttered.

'C'mon, I ain't no coward, neither are you, but we've got our women to think of. I ain't throwing my life away for you pa's ranch or Sykes' law.'

'You're making one big mistake here, Sykes,' MacPherson was saying. 'This is my town. Every last plank, every last grain of dirt on the sidewalk and every last person.' He narrowed his eyes. 'And I can see those of you who betray me. You'd better leave now, 'cos once I've got my town back, it ain't going to go well for you.'

Pastor Sims spurred his horse up level with the marshal. 'That's enough, MacPherson,' he shouted. 'You may own land and business, but the people are God's and you got no rights over them.'

'You're sacked, Pastor, never liked

your sermons much, anyway,' MacPherson gurgled a laugh.

'Give yourself up to the marshal, it'll go better for you,' persisted Sims.

'Give yourself up, MacPherson,' called Hunter. 'I guarantee you the best defence attorney in the land — me.'

MacPherson fiddled with the reins pushing them into his left hand.

'I see what you're doing,' said Sykes. 'Don't think of pulling your gun.'

A man David recognized as MacPherson's foreman brought his horse up to the front now. 'Maybe things ain't quite like you think they are, Boss,' he suggested. 'Maybe we should all back off a bit and talk it over. What with Paulie being dead, and them three gunslingers you hired buying it, maybe this ain't the way to sort things out.'

'You're fired too!' shouted MacPherson. 'Get out of my sight. I don't pay you to advise me or to whinge.'

'Sounded like sense — ' began the pastor, but the force of MacPherson's bullet sent him right over the back of his horse. Then, as Flynn predicted, it got messy.

Sykes was firing both his pistols, but his horse was wheeling round, and he wasn't hitting anything. The pastor's horse, now riderless, was barging about, and getting tangled up with everyone else. Flynn, for all his talk, didn't run for cover at all, but got stuck in, taking on two of MacPherson's men and chasing them off, their heart not being in the fight anyway.

David rode over to Pastor Sims, but he was clearly dead; the shot, at short range, had ripped open his chest. Then two of MacPherson's men were galloping towards him. He fired back, and clipped the flank of one of their horses. He saw the other man aim his rifle. David squeezed the trigger of his revolver and the man fell over the pommel as his horse ran off.

Suddenly there was even more gunfire and shouting coming from the town. It was the hands from the River

Bow, firing into the air, their presence enough to make the rest of MacPherson's men decide to call it a day.

David swirled his horse round and round. He couldn't see Caroline; that was good. His father and Hunter seemed unharmed, but Sykes had taken a bullet in his side, though he was still trying to shoot MacPherson. Seeing his men desert him, MacPherson turned his attention from his enemies and galloped after his hands, shouting the vilest obscenities. That gave David his chance, he pushed his horse fast after him, calling MacPherson's name. Then he was aware of another horse beside him, it was Mark.

'I don't want to shoot him in the back,' he called over to his father.

'I don't want him getting away, either. I'm not going through all this again,' panted Mark. He aimed at MacPherson's horse, dust coming up from round its hoofs as he missed.

MacPherson pivoted his horse round, but his left hand was all but useless, and as he had to use his right to steady his mount, his gun span from his hand.

'Got him!' cried Mark, holstering his own weapon and barrelling his horse into the side of MacPherson's. Both men fell to the ground, and they began to grapple, but Mark was bigger and uninjured and soon he bettered MacPherson and pulled him to his feet, gripping both his hands behind him.

Sykes slithered down from his saddle and passed the handcuffs to Mark. 'Connor MacPherson, consider yourself arrested,' he said.

MacPherson was still fighting hard, his feet kicked up dust and he managed to free his right arm, which swept out in a flash and whipped one of Sykes' guns from its holster.

'You're going to lose everything, Merkel!' screamed MacPherson, his lips white with spittle. Hunter appeared from nowhere, but attempting to throw himself from his horse onto MacPherson, he managed to pull down Mark.

The pistol swung around dangerously, firing indiscriminately. Then MacPherson stopped. He looked up at David, who was still mounted. A smile twitched at the sides of his mouth. 'You watching this, Merkel!' he spat as he lined up his gun.

David felt his horse rear up beneath him, and somewhere, far away in the distance, he heard a gun firing and his father calling his name.

16

'Can't remember the last time I wore a dress,' said Louisa, lifting the hem of her skirt as they climbed the few steps onto the porch of the ranch house. 'Think I'll change back to pants as soon as it's decent to. How long after a funeral should I wait, do you think?'

Caroline was wearing the dark plain travelling suit she had worn for her journey to Arizona. It felt strange to be back in her familiar clothes, yet right, somehow, as her stay must end soon. 'I'm not sure there's any rules about a girl wearing pants and bereavement,' she said.

'You cried a lot, Caro,' said Louisa, pushing open the wide front door. 'Meat smells like it's cooking fine.'

'Yes,' said Caroline, following her into the kitchen. 'I was fond of Paulie. And, though I only knew Pastor Sims a

283

day, I felt a fondness for him too. I suppose it was the way of his death, trying to do the right thing, that was so tragic. His wife spoke movingly, didn't she? I think I was crying for her more than him, really. What do you do when the one you love dies?'

'In Pa's case you take to the bottle. Can't see Mrs Sims following the same route, though.'

Caroline shook her head. 'Go and put your pants on, Miss Merkel,' she said with a smile.

'I ain't that bad,' said Louisa, 'I really would have liked Pastor Sims to marry me and Flynn.'

'You heard Marshal Sykes say he'll send a man up from Carlyle — you'll still get married.'

They heard someone calling from outside.

It was Hunter. 'Hello, ladies,' he called, 'I'm having some trouble getting out of this buggy with my crutches.'

Caroline ran down the steps and helped him down.

'Damn nuisance, this sprain,' he said, 'but the doctor's insistent I'm not to put weight on it for another two weeks.'

'Well, if you must go throwing yourself off horses,' said Caroline.

'Thank you so much for coming,' said Louisa, hugging him. 'We want to give you a good send-off.'

'And I thought I'd better see what I'm investing in before I go back East.' He looked up. 'It's a grand house.'

'Course it is,' laughed Louisa. 'We've got a bathroom and a flushing water closet, you know. What were you expecting, a log cabin?'

'Ah,' said Hunter, 'I fear I was.'

Once inside Hunter gratefully sank into a chair, and Louisa found a footstool upon which he could rest his injured leg.

'I think we gave Paulie and the pastor a good send-off,' he said. 'And nice to see you two ladies so smartly attired.'

'How have things been in town?' asked Caroline.

'You mean, how is Davy,' he said with

a knowing smile. 'Why did you avoid him at the funeral?'

She shrugged. 'It was busy, and Lou and I were keen to get back.'

'Well he's fine. He and Elijah have been working hard, rounding up as many of MacPherson's men as they can, taking witness statements and preparing the cases. I've been closely involved with him. I like the way that sharp mind of his works; he's bright enough to be a lawyer, you know. And la Bute, knowing he'll swing for Paulie, has finally told us exactly what happened to Dancing Bird. I think Davy's very persistent questioning wore him down in the end. Apparently la Bute had travelled back from Mint Creek overnight. In the early hours of the morning, as he passed by the ranch on his way back to town, he'd seen Dancing Bird. Frustrated that he hadn't discovered any gold, la Bute beat the whereabouts out of the poor old man and killed him to keep the secret safe.'

'How did he know it was the stolen

gold, and not just gold in the river?' asked Caroline.

'Dancing Bird said he'd found 'pure gold'. Knowing his partners had hidden the proceeds of their crime around here, la Bute put two and two together. Then, of course, as sheriff he was called in to investigate the murder. He wasn't clever enough to plant the evidence against Caleb, but was cunning enough to use it when it appeared. Anyway, I think Davy's satisfied he'll see justice done.'

'That deputy's badge burns awfully brightly on his chest,' said Louisa, 'do you think he'll come back to us?'

Hunter smiled. 'Judge Frixell's holding a special court next week, as soon as all the prisoners have been taken to Carlyle. Once Davy's seen la Bute and MacPherson stand trial, he'll come back. Though in the case of MacPherson, I'll be pleading insanity. The man should be in an asylum.'

Louisa snorted. 'I don't know why you're defending him, let the mad man rot in jail or hang.'

Hunter sighed. 'I suppose I feel I sort of promised him I would.'

'You're too honourable, Hunter,' said Caroline. 'Anyway, I've decided I'll go back East with you. I know we'll be in Carlyle a while, because of the trials, but I don't mind.'

'You crossed a continent alone to be with that man, my dear, why give up now?'

'David's intentions have always been clear, and he keeps nearly being killed. I'm not sure my nerves can stand much more.'

Louisa shivered. 'If Davy's horse hadn't reared and taken the bullet Connor meant for him . . . ' Her voice trailed off.

'Well it did, and Davy was unharmed,' said Hunter. 'You've got till tomorrow to decide what to do, Caroline. You know my feelings on the subject, but it's up to you.'

'See, Caro,' said Louisa, 'Hunter wants you to stay as well. We need you.

If me and Pa are left on our own, well, you know what happens.'

'Talk to Davy tonight,' said Hunter.

'He's coming?' exclaimed Louisa.

'Well of course he is. I want all my friends at my farewell party. Now, would you young ladies get one of those strong men who work here, to lift two crates of champagne, packed in ice, from the back of my buggy? We have friends to mourn and new beginnings to celebrate. I find champagne perfect for both occasions.'

★   ★   ★

Everyone at River Bow was invited to the ranch house for the meal. David had brought Marshal Sykes with him. The law man was keen to talk about the events of the previous week, the injury he'd sustained and the number of stitches the doctor had to put in his side. David was popular too; everyone wanted to know what was happening in town and how many prisoners would be going to Carlyle. Once or twice Caroline got close to him, but within seconds he managed to move away from her.

After the gunfight he'd been knocked out, falling from his horse. As he came round he'd been happy enough to hold her hand, but as soon as he fully regained his senses he became completely cold to her. Colder than at any time since she'd been in Arizona. It was as if he'd decided to make one last determined effort to alienate her, and it worked.

*   *   *

Excitement, fuelled by Hunter's champagne, made for a noisy party. When all the food had finally been consumed Mark tapped on the table and stood up.

'This is it!' he declared, holding aloft a piece of paper. 'Every last penny paid off. River Bow Ranch is safe. Thank you, thank you all.'

Caroline started to clap and soon

everyone had burst into applause.

'Make sure everyone's glass is full,' said Mark to his daughter. He held his glass in front of him and they all stood up. 'It's been difficult. A long hard slog, and the women have worked just as hard as the men, and with rather less complaining, I venture.' There was a ripple of soft laughter and agreement. 'Miss Caroline Fisher, I doubt when you got on the train in Vermont you ever thought you'd be taking part in a cattle drive or coming under attack from gunslingers, did you, my dear?'

'I did not. The last few weeks have been something of an experience.' She shot a swift glance at David. He was looking straight ahead.

'Huh, just wish you were calling me 'Pa',' grumbled Mark.

David put down his glass and turned away.

'Not my business what the young people get up to,' Mark muttered under his breath. 'Today I want to drink to the ranch,' he continued aloud. 'But our success wasn't achieved without loss. Let's not forget those who aren't with us, but should be. My darling wife Mary, Dancing Bird, Paulie MacPherson, and Pastor Sims.'

They all looked down in silence for a moment.

'River Bow!' shouted Mark.

'River Bow!' everyone responded.

'Can we dance?' asked Louisa.

'Surely we can,' said Mark.

Olly went to get his fiddle while Louisa and Flynn moved the furniture to the walls. They were the first to begin dancing, when Olly, accompanied by Caleb on his little Jew's harp, began to play. Emboldened by liquor, Stumpy bravely asked Caroline for a dance, which she eagerly accepted.

* * *

David went out onto the porch. The air was even hotter outside. He looked up at the stars and, in the dark blue sky, he could still make out the distant mountains. The music stopped for a moment, then another tune started off. He didn't need to turn round to know that Caroline had joined him.

'Your father has claimed Stumpy for the next dance, I'm not sure if I should be worried,' she said.

He could hear amusement in her voice, tinged with something else, desperation? 'They've known each other a long time, and you leaving the room has reduced the available female partners by fifty per cent,' he said.

She leaned on the rail. 'I do love this place, in a strange way.'

'Don't get too fond. It's time you went back to Vermont.'

'I know. I'm taking the stage with Hunter.'

'I'll be glad to see you go.' He felt a heel talking to her like that, but what was the point in raising false hopes?

'Yes, David. I'd hoped we could . . . well, you know . . . '

'That was never going to happen.'

She swallowed hard. 'I see that now.

293

Your life is at River Bow, they'd never manage without you. I wouldn't want you to go back to the bank. Everything here is so alive.'

He slapped his neck. 'Alive with flies, snakes, coyotes, and yes, gunslingers and villains of every kind.' He stopped and breathed heavily for a while. 'When I worked for your father I knew what every day would be like. No surprises. I had it all planned, we would marry, have our own house and raise our children. We'd expand our business, open more branches and one day I'd take over from your father. Now, I can't see the future. Oh, I know we've got the trials coming up, but after that it's just a blank. A thick blank wall I can see neither under, nor over, nor through. I don't know if I like it, but I know I have to be here.'

'You like it.' Once again there was a silence between them, and though not intimate neither was there any animosity. She knew she didn't want to leave him; even this, with no fondness

294

between them was better than being apart. 'Louisa wants me to stay, she has an idea,' she said at last.

'Spare me,' he snapped.

'It is a proposition, and a very practical proposition, actually. You're all going to be busy building up the ranch and Louisa has neither the talent nor the disposition to run the house. I have both. I don't have to go back. I could stay and be housekeeper. I will never mention the feelings I have for you — our relationship will be professional. Let me stay for six months. Write it down in your diary, you like efficiency. Six months exactly. You know my feelings well, and they will not change. If during that time you feel — '

'I shall not,' he snapped. She was so close, he hardly had to stretch and he could touch her, feel the warmth of her skin, and if he did that he would never want to let her go. 'I shall not change my mind, Caroline, so why waste six months of your life.'

'They will not be wasted. Do we have

a deal? Shall we shake on it?'

He turned his back on her. 'No. Catch the stage with Hunter.'

'Very well. We'll say goodbye in the morning shall we?'

'Yes. Goodbye, then, tomorrow.' He heard her go back into the house.

He leaned against one of the wooden posts, his breath raw and ragged. It was the smell of Hunter's cigar, rather than the tapping of his crutches on the boards that alerted him that he had company. 'You'll see her safely home, won't you?' he said, desperately hoping Hunter couldn't hear the despair in his voice.

'No.'

'What?'

'I don't think Miss Fisher's going anywhere for a while.'

David thumped the rail. 'Damn you, Hunter. Will you never give up! I promised myself. I will not break that promise.'

Hunter took a long pull on his cigar. 'Breaking a promise made to yourself isn't the worst thing you can do. Especially if it was a damn fool promise in the first place. It's up to you, of course, whether you decide to ruin two lives on a matter of principle, or do the right thing.' He paused. He could hear David desperately gulping air. 'I counted, it took me twenty steps to get from the parlour to here, and that's me, a fat old man on crutches. It'll take you, with your long, young legs a lot less. You know where those few short steps would take you, don't you.'

'The parlour,' said David with a sneer.

Hunter ignored that. 'Happiness, that's where you'd be headed. If you're brave enough.'

'So you're accusing me of cowardice now, are you?'

Hunter chuckled softly. 'Sounds like I am.'

'Damn you, damn you, Hunter.' David rushed down the steps and into the yard.

Hunter looked through the window at the gathering inside. He could hear the music and the laughter. Mark was dancing with Caroline. She was smiling, but he could see the sadness she tried to hide beneath her bright expression. Hunter didn't move as he heard footsteps coming up the stairs and going into the house. His heart beating fast, he moved closer to the window. David came into the room, he saw him walk straight over to his father and whisper something in his ear. Mark relinquished his partner with delight, and then David's arm was right where it should be, around Caroline's waist. Their cheeks touched and their fingers entwined.

Hunter took a long, contented pull on his cigar. 'Damn me, indeed,' he said to himself. 'If they don't call their first son Hunter, I'll sue.'

THE END